THE KEEPER
OF DARKNESS

By

Ladean Warner

*Carol,
Enjoy the book!
God bliss,
Ladean*

PublishAmerica
Baltimore

First printing

All characters in this book are fictitious, and any resemblance to real persons, living or dead, is coincidental.

PublishAmerica has allowed this work to remain exactly as the author intended, verbatim, without editorial input.

Scripture taken from the HOLY BIBLE, NEW INTERNATIONAL VERSION®. Copyright © 1973, 1978, 1984 International Bible Society. Used by permission of Zondervan. All rights reserved.

The "NIV" and "New Internation Version" trademarks are registered in the United States Patent and Trademark Office by International Bible Society. Use of either trademark requires permission of International Bible Society.

Sites, E. (1876) *Trusting Jesus*. Retrieved from: http://www.cyberhymnal.org/htm/t/r/trusting.htm

ISBN: 1-60703-743-2
PUBLISHED BY PUBLISHAMERICA, LLLP
www.publishamerica.com
Baltimore

Printed in the United States of America

CHAPTER 1

The dark blue Toyota kept pace with the other cars as it headed up the Northway out of Albany. The only benefit for the late hour was not being caught with the other commuters in the rush hour traffic. Kathy Stanwick dreaded the long drive to Granelle just outside of Saratoga Springs. When she moved into the house last year, she considered the drive a small price to pay for the peace she felt in the country.

It had been a long day and Kathy could still feel the tension. The client was being difficult and she wondered if the extra hours she put in tonight would pay off in the presentation tomorrow. Her job was on the line and she knew that this was her last chance. Kathy still hadn't told her husband, George, about her problems at work. Not only did they have a new mortgage, but two car payments and other debts.

Kathy kept replaying her presentation in her mind, blocking out the music playing on the radio. She sighed knowing that she was in for a long night. As she reached her exit, she turned off the air conditioner and opened the window letting the warm air blow across her face. Strands of her long brown hair blew across her face and she brushed them out of her dark brown eyes. It had been a long hot summer and the remains could still be felt in the air on this mid-October evening.

As Kathy turned down Church Street that would take her away from Saratoga toward her house, she caught a glimpse of a shadow in her rearview mirror. When she stopped for the light in front of the hospital, she stared in the mirror trying to figure out what she had seen. She reached over and rolled up the window as a stab of uncertain fear gnawed at her stomach. As the light turned green, she eased through the intersection still looking around for the cause of her fears. Reaching the outskirts of the city, the street narrowed and she lost the comfort of the streetlights. Dusk was making everything look like deep shadows and Kathy turned on her headlights.

Blaming her unease on tomorrow's presentation, Kathy let her mind drift back to her work. She turned off the main street and onto a narrow dirt road that would take her to Granelle. Driving past the occasional houses of her unknown neighbors, she glanced over at her briefcase on the seat next to her. Kathy screamed jerking the steering wheel to the left as a bat flew into the passenger window. The front left tire hit the softer dirt on the shoulder of the road and she jerked the wheel to the right and slammed on the brakes to keep from sliding into the ravine. The car came to an abrupt stop and she hit her head on the steering wheel.

With shaking hands, Kathy touched her head where a welt was already forming. She looked back to the passenger window and the darkness of the woods looked back at her. Glancing out the windows around her, she only saw the woods and the darkness of the night. She let out her breath, eased off on the brakes, and straightened the car.

Reaching her driveway, Kathy stopped and looked up the long driveway to her empty dark house. She let the car slowly ease forward as she looked around her. The woods surrounding her property seemed to be full of menace. Her head throbbed where she hit it and her heart was racing. She reached over and opened the glove box to get the automatic garage door opener.

Punching the button, the light from the garage spilled into the driveway as the door slowly rose. As Kathy slid the car into the garage, she punched the button again to let the door close and turned off her headlights. Shutting the car off, she sat in the car feeling the tension leave. She closed her eyes and laid her head back as she willed herself to relax. The light bulb exploded showering the car in broken glass. A low growling sound filled the dark garage. Kathy sat looking toward the front of the car where the sound seemed to be coming from.

Moving slowly, Kathy reached out and touched the keys hanging from the ignition. The car moved with the weight as something began to climb onto the hood of the car. She couldn't make out the shape of the dark shadow and she wasn't sure she wanted to. Kathy turned the key and jammed the car into drive. The car lunged forward and the creature slid off the car. Kathy put the car into reverse and slammed into the garage door. She reached down next to her for the garage door opener and couldn't find it. The creature was back on its feet and coming back at the car. Kathy put the car back into drive and stepped on the gas. The creature seemed to sense her actions and disappeared to the right as her car hit the wall.

6

As she looked around, Kathy felt around for the garage door opener. She caught movement in the rearview mirror and threw the car into reverse hitting the door again. Glass fell onto the trunk as one of the garage door windows broke. The creature flew at the driver's door and Kathy dove away across the seat knocking her briefcase and purse on the floor. The contents of her purse spilled and Kathy fumbled for her cell phone. She dialed 911 as the creature continued its assault on the driver's door. As she listened to the ringing of the phone, she searched the floor for the garage door opener again.

As the dispatcher answered the 911 call, Kathy looked up at the passenger window and realized to her horror that there was another creature in the garage. She screamed as the passenger door slowly began to open.

CHAPTER 2

Jake Peterson walked into the emergency room at Saratoga Hospital and looked around. At 2:30 in the morning, the waiting room was empty. A tired nurse looked up from a desk behind a glass enclosure. Jake walked over and she slid open the window at the desk.

"What are you here for?" she asked.

Jake cleared his throat. "I got a call that Walter Ryerson was brought in."

"Are you a relative?"

"No. Um…" he hesitated. "I'm a minister."

The nurse looked at him suspiciously. Jake certainly didn't look like a minister. The dark blue shirt he was wearing complimented his blond hair and blue eyes. Jake was handsome, but didn't seem to know it.

"You got some proof?"

"Proof? That I'm a minister?"

"Yes. Like a card or ID. Most ministers don't act all nervous like you. Besides, I've seen you some place and it wasn't in church," she said.

Jake pulled out his wallet. "Well, I am a minister. It's just that I'm a new minister. Pastor Ryerson is the senior pastor at my church," he explained as he searched through his wallet. He pulled out a little white card that showed he was an ordained minister.

The nurse looked at the card and then back at him making Jake uncomfortable. "Jake Peterson? I know this name." She stared at him a little longer and handed the card back to him.

"Satisfied?" Jake asked, taking his card.

"No. Stay here. I'm going to check you out. You're someone else and I don't know why you're really here."

When she left, Jake sighed. It was all new to him and his first hospital call was for the senior pastor where he just became the associate pastor two months before. He went to the door that separated the waiting room from the

ER and peaked through a small window. To the one side was the nurse's station. The bay to the ambulance entrance was at his right. Jake saw a police officer standing inside the door and waved to him. The man recognized Jake and opened the door.

"Hey, Peterson," the officer said shaking Jake's hand. "What brings you to the ER in the middle of the night? Thought you gave up this kind of work."

"Guess emergencies happen in my new job too. How have you been Crandall?" Jake asked.

"Pretty good. I just passed the sergeant's exam. Looks like I'm getting out of Granelle," Steve Crandall responded.

"That's great. How's Bennett?"

"Ornery as ever. You remember Ralph Walker?"

"He was the janitor at the station. Right?"

"That's him. Got sent to jail for domestic violence."

"And just what do you think you are doing in here, Detective Peterson?" the nurse came from behind him demanding.

Jake put up his hands in mock defensiveness. "Honest, I'm a minister now. Just ask this officer. I'm not on the force anymore."

"That's right lady," Steve said.

"No, you're that detective that solved those big cases a few years back. You were always on the news."

"Yes, that was me. But I left law enforcement and I'm now a minister. I'm here for Pastor Walt. His wife called me."

She stood with her hands on her hips, eyes narrowed. A doctor came behind the nurse. "Well, Detective Peterson. Are you here for the Murphy boy?"

Jake shook hands with the doctor. "Dr. Martin, it's good to see you. No, I'm not here on police business. Like I was just telling the nurse, I'm a minister now."

"What a shame. You were a good cop," the doctor said shaking his head.

"I'm here about Pastor Ryerson. Is he here?" Jake said.

"Yes, he is in Room 4. It's a real shame, though," he said shaking his head.

Jake felt a jolt of fear. "Is he alright? His wife called me before the ambulance came."

"I'm sorry. I didn't mean Mr. Ryerson. You. It's a shame about you. You were such a good cop. You could have made it big."

"Well, thanks Doc. But what about Pastor Ryerson? Can I see him?"

"Oh sure, sure. You know where Room 4 is. Go on in."

Jake walked down the hall to the room and saw the nurse trying to look busy scowling at him. Jake felt like smiling, but saw Walt first and stopped just outside the door. He looked so old to Jake. The vibrant minister that preached so fervently now lay in the sterile hospital bed. His eyes were closed and he was hooked up to monitors. Jake knew that Walt was in his upper fifties, but didn't look it. He had a head of black wavy hair and vibrant brown eyes. Walt was known all over town because he loved to walk and talked to everyone he saw. Jake wondered how this man could be laying in the hospital bed.

Jake stepped into the room and saw Millie in a chair at the side of the bed. Unlike her husband, Millie looked her age with her grey short hair and her soft blue eyes. All the children in the church called her Grandma Millie. She was holding Walt's hand and her eyes were closed too. But Jake could see her mouth moving in silent prayer. Quietly, Jake slipped over behind her and laid his hands on her shoulders. She looked up at Jake and her smile looked strained and tired. Concern was etched in her face. To Jake, they both looked like they had aged overnight.

"Thanks for coming out in the middle of the night," she said getting to her feet. She reached up and hugged Jake.

"How's Walt?" Jake asked as he gave her a hug back.

Millie sat back down and reached out for Walt's hand. "He's not very good. He had a heart attack. The doctor wants him transported to St. John's Hospital in Albany so he can have a catheter done. He may need open heart surgery. Even so, his first concern was for the church, for the people. That's why I called you. He wanted me to call you even before I called for the ambulance. Of course, I didn't."

"Millie, it's going to be alright. St. John's is a great hospital for heart problems. He will get good care and I'll stay here as long as you need me."

"It's just the church…"

"Let's be concerned about Walt first," Jake started.

Millie shook her head. "You don't understand the way it is, Jake. When Walt and I came to this church, it became our lives. The people mean so much to us. So many of them have problems and concerns. They depend on us to pray for them and to help them. We knew we were getting older. That's why Walt decided to hire an associate pastor. He felt in time, you could take over the church. But it's too soon…."

10

Jake put his hand on her shoulder and stopped her. "Millie, God led me to this church and this ministry. I'll be there for the people. You be there for Walt."

Millie stopped talking and sighed. Closing her eyes, she went back to her prayers. Jake didn't know if what he said helped Millie. It sure didn't convince him that he could handle the problems at the church. Jake had just graduated from seminary in June and spent the summer at his parent's home in New Jersey while seeking an associate pastor position. When the friend that lead him to the Lord told him that Granelle Gospel was beginning a search for an associate pastor, he felt that God led him back to Granelle.

But as Jake stood in the hospital room staring down at Walt, he felt unsure of his ability to lead the church. This was something he never felt as a cop. Seeing another chair in the corner, Jake sat down and began to pray. Ten minutes later, a nurse came in and told them the ambulance won't be able to come until the morning. But the doctor would be in soon to talk to them.

Walt opened his eyes and saw that Jake was there and motioned him over to the bed. Jake reached down and Walt griped his hand tightly.

"Jake," he whispered. "Call Mrs. Baxter to get the prayer chain going. You need a prayer cover to get through this."

"I know Walt," Jake said. "I'll take care of everything. You just get better."

"You don't understand. Something is happening…."

"Excuse me," the doctor interrupted. "Can I talk to the Ryersons in private?"

The old pastor shook his head, but didn't argue. He dropped Jake's hand and closed his eyes again. Jake stepped out of the room, but could still hear the doctor explaining the problem with transporting him down to Albany.

As the doctor left, Millie came into the hall and patted Jake's arm. "The ambulance won't be able to get here until about 7:00 in the morning. Why don't you go on home?"

"Millie, what do you think Walt was talking about?"

"I think it's just the illness. Go home and get some sleep."

"Don't you want me to go with you down to St. John's?"

"No, my daughter lives in Albany. She's going to meet us at the hospital. You get some sleep. The people need you to be strong."

"Can I pray with you before I leave?"

Millie smiled and nodded. They bowed their heads together and held hands while Jake prayed for Walt.

CHAPTER 3

Reggie Bennett is the best captain that had ever run the small Granelle police department. Reggie got his experience the hard way working downstate in the city. When he was offered the promotion and the opportunity to work in Saratoga County, he jumped at the chance to work in the quiet country hamlet of Granelle. It was a chance to get his wife and two sons out away from the city life.

Reggie is a big burly black man that could intimidate suspects and police alike. He was over 6' tall and worked out at the local gym. He had been a big fan of James Earl Jones when he was in high school and honed his voice to sound like Jones. Reggie found the deep booming voice came in handy in police work.

He sat in the unmarked police car next to Jake's truck and watched Jake walk out of the hospital into the October night. As Jake walked over to his truck, Reggie opened the door and got out.

"Captain?" Jake asked surprised.

"Crandall told me you were here," Reggie said. "I've wanted to talk to you since you got back in town."

"So, you have your cops hunting me down in the middle of the night?" Jake said good-naturedly.

"Your name came up in an investigation we have been conducting. I mentioned that it would be good to talk to you about it. So, Crandall called and let me know you were here."

"Okay, so why did you have to find me?"

"We had another victim tonight. I want you to come to the crime scene."

"Crime scene? Captain, I'm not on the force anymore."

"You don't think I know that," Reggie said gruffly. "You were the best detective I ever worked with. I need your help on this one, Jake. Consider it a consulting job."

"Any other time and I'd be flattered. But Pastor Ryerson is going to be on his way to Albany in the morning. I need to take over the responsibilities at the church. I don't even know what that all involves yet. But I know I've got a sermon to prepare for in four days."

"I know that you have a new boss and I respect the decision you made, but this is the second victim," Reggie hesitated. "Granelle is a small town and big crimes affect everyone, not just the cops."

"Captain."

"Jake you don't work for me anymore. Just call me Reggie."

"Okay, Reggie," Jake said unlocking his truck door. He reached in for his black leather jacket and slipped it on. "It's just that…"

The radio in the police car paged Reggie.

Reggie sat down in the car and picked up the mic. "What's up Marty?"

"They need you back at the Stanwicks," the dispatcher said. "They found something strange."

"Alright. Let them know I'm on my way."

Jake stood listening, concern etched on his face. "The only Stanwicks I know in Granelle are George and Kathy. Is that the crime scene?"

Reggie stood back up. "Yeah. What do you know about them?"

"I know that they are members of my church and they come every Sunday."

"They go to Granelle Gospel?"

"Yes. George helps out with some of the maintenance during the week."

"You can go with me on official business of the church. If you find out anything that can be useful in the investigation, we can talk," Reggie said getting excited.

Jake put up his hand shaking his head. "If I'm there on church business, anything that I find out would be considered confidential. I would be there as a pastor and counselor. And don't start in with telling me anything about withholding evidence, Captain, I know that law too."

"But you will go over with me?"

"I'll go, but as their pastor."

"Okay," Reggie said smiling. "Get in and we can talk about the case."

"I'll drive my own vehicle and I prefer not to know about the case. I'm there for them in the capacity of their pastor, remember that."

CHAPTER 4

Jake slowly drove up Kathy Stanwick's driveway behind Reggie's police car glancing at the isolation of the house. He pulled his truck behind the police cruiser and shut it off. He sat in his truck taking in the scene before him. The garage door was bowed out and one of the windows had been broken. Yellow police tape blocked anyone from opening the garage door. Jake saw Meg Riley step out of a side door and approach two uniformed policemen who were looking at something in the shrubs near the door.

Jake drew in his breath at the sight of Meg. He fell in love with her the day she joined the squad and spilled her coffee on him. They began to date and quickly planned a future together that ended when Jake came to the Lord. He had tried to talk to her about God, but she wanted nothing to do with God or the church. He knew that Meg was now engaged to a hotshot lawyer in Albany. In spite of all the changes and years apart, Jake still missed Meg.

Jake got out of the truck and saw the smug look on Reggie's face. Jake shook his head at him, "Why didn't you mention that Meg would be here?"

"Would you have come if I told you?"

"I would have come for the Stanwicks. Just probably in the morning."

"You didn't leave law enforcement for God. You left because of Riley."

Jake stared at Reggie and then shook his head again. "That's not true. I felt like God called me into ministry."

Reggie shrugged. "If that's the truth, then what's the problem?"

"I don't want to hurt her again."

"Hurt her or hurt you?" Reggie asked jabbing his finger in Jake's chest.

Meg looked toward the driveway as the voices drifted in the still night. Even in the semi-darkness, she knew it was Jake and walked to meet them out of earshot from the other policemen. She noticed Jake was wearing the blue shirt she bought him for his birthday several years ago.

"Captain, we have some evidence you need to see," Meg said in a professional voice, not acknowledging Jake. Meg looked dwarfed between the two tall men. They walked back toward the house with Meg between them. Jake looked into the window at the smashed up car. Several portable lights were shining on the car and another detective was looking in the front seat of the car. Bloodstains were splattered on the floor and wall.

"How bad is the victim?" Jake asked.

Meg looked into the window and watched as her partner, Pete Burgess, picked up a garage door opener and put it into an evidence bag. Looking back at Reggie she said, "Captain, I don't think it is appropriate for a civilian to be here at a crime scene."

"What isn't appropriate, Detective Riley, is for you to be questioning your boss. Besides, Pastor Peterson is here for the family. He is their minister."

"Oh, sorry sir," Meg said shuffling her feet. "Perhaps you should see what Burgess found in the car sir. Then the pastor can go see Mr. Stanwick," she added glaring at Jake. Jake looked down into her deep green eyes, he felt his heart break a little. He noticed that she had let her short blond hair grow out to her shoulders and it softened her. Jake looked away quickly hoping she hadn't noticed his interest.

"Has the victim been taken to the hospital?" Jake asked.

Meg looked at Reggie and sighed, "That's part of the problem, Captain. We can't find the victim."

Jake looked down at Meg again, but she continued talking to Reggie. "Lots of blood in the car, but no victim. So that means no body. That's why I asked dispatch to call you. We can't find Mrs. Stanwick."

"I already knew that Riley. That's why Jake is here," Reggie said.

"I'm sorry for questioning you Captain. But this isn't right. Peterson is no longer on the force and to have him here…." She stopped and crossed her arms, a gesture Jake knew all too well.

"And if you recall Riley, this is the second scene without a body," Reggie turned to Jake. "And that is why I wanted you here. Martha Rowley disappeared last week and now Kathy Stanwick. Do you remember those cases you worked on several years ago where there were no bodies?"

"Yeah, I was just thinking about them. But we solved those cases. Douglas Vincent Angelos is doing life for the murders."

"But with the same MO, there is always the possibility of a connection. Maybe a copycat," Reggie said. "Then there is always the possibility that there was a mistake. Maybe Angelos didn't murder those other women."

Jake felt himself getting defensive and stepped away from the garage door. "Look. I've got to see if George needs anything." He turned and started toward the front of the house. Reggie grabbed his arm and forced him to stop.

"Will you at least come and look?"

"I have a lot of respect for you, Captain. But I'm not a detective anymore. I've got to see if George needs anything. I just want to pray with him for his wife. Okay?"

Meg made a disgusted sound. "You got a problem Riley?" Reggie asked her.

"I've already told you my objections. Besides, I'm the lead on this case and you should be talking about your theories with me. Jake can't add anything to the old cases that I don't already know. I know that he had doubts about Angelos. I also can get the old case files if we need to. Why don't you trust me to handle this?"

"I want you to think about something," Reggie said. "I was there when those women disappeared and when Angelos was arrested. Jake told me that he thought that it might have been a mistake. Yeah, Angelos had a connection to each of them, but it was all circumstantial evidence. There were no bodies and no murder weapons. Jake built the whole case against him. But it was all Jake, not you. And there is a lot that Jake knows instinctively that you won't find in any case files."

Jake interrupted turning to Reggie. "Reggie, I need you to understand that I came back to Granelle because I care about the people here. I want to do the work that God called me here to do. I can't get back in the middle of police work, especially not now with Pastor Walt in the hospital. The people need me."

"That's right the people need you to help find whoever has taken these women. There is no way, looking at that crime scene, that Kathy Stanwick is alive."

"The people need me as a spiritual advisor not as a cop."

"I'm not asking you to be a cop again. I'm asking you to just see the scene, tell me what you think. I need to know if it's the same."

"I'm sorry Reggie, but I can't. Meg is a good cop. Let her do her job and let me do mine. I really should get in and talk to George."

Jake turned and walked around the side of the house. Once he knew he was alone, he looked up at the sky. Closing his eyes, he whispered, "Dear Lord, why did you bring me back to Granelle? Especially now? How can I lead the church? How can I turn my back on the department? I need You. Please give me the answers."

The silence of the night was the only answer that Jake received. He stared out into the darkness of the woods. Jake turned and walked up to the front door.

Jake rang the doorbell and an older woman answered. "Yes," she asked politely.

"I'm Pastor Jake, from Granelle Gospel. I heard what happened with Kathy and I came to see if there was anything I could do for George."

"Well, thank you for coming by Pastor, but I'm his mother. We don't need any other outsiders here...."

"Pastor Jake," George said coming up behind his mother. George was a tall thin man with black curly hair. He had his mother's dark brown eyes. But that's where the resemblance ended. "Please come in. Mother, please let my minster come in."

Jake stepped into the living room. "What happened George?" Jake asked in concern as George's mother left the room in a huff.

"I don't know. I came home from work and found the garage like that. I looked all around the house and could tell Kathy never came in. The police haven't told me anything yet."

"I'm sure they will talk to you soon. I see that there are people searching in the woods already."

"Yes, my father and brother are out there. The police asked me to stay here for now. I want to be out there looking with them. I heard there is another woman missing too. Do you think there is a connection?"

"The police will explore all the possibilities."

"I'm actually surprised to see you. Did Pastor Walt ask you to come over?"

Jake shook his head. "Pastor Walt is at the hospital. He had a heart attack. I was up there visiting him when I heard about Kathy. I came right over."

"I'm sorry to hear about Pastor Walt. Is he okay?"

"He may need surgery. You know, why don't we pray together for Kathy and Pastor Walt?"

"I'd like that. Let's sit on the couch. Mother, would you like to pray with us?"

"I'm busy right now," his mother called out from the other room. The two men sat on the couch together and began to pray. Mrs. Stanwick looked out from the kitchen and scowled. She didn't understand her son's fanatical ways.

Dawn was just breaking as Jake walked back to his truck. He felt like he was being watched. He knew that the woods were full of people searching for Kathy. When he got to his truck, he turned back to look, but no one was there. He could hear some of the searchers in the woods, but they weren't in sight. But the feeling of being watched stayed with him and even made him feel uneasy. He glanced around him at the dusky shadows and sensed something wrong. A movement caught his eye half way down the driveway, but Jake couldn't tell what it was.

Jake walked to the back of his truck keeping his eyes on the area where he saw movement. It appeared that one spot was darker than the rest. An old familiar feeling crept over him. Jake stood still watching for movement again, but there was nothing. He took a step away from his truck and a low growling sound started behind him. He swung around and saw nothing.

The growling stopped. Jake tried to shake the fear as he walked to the driver's side of the truck. A movement to his left caught him off guard and he hollered. He heard the sound of something rushing away and turned to see undergrowth of the woods moving where something had just run through it. Jake heard shouting coming from the woods and took a few steps toward the house. He could hear someone call his name and the footsteps of the officers running toward him. Still, he concentrated on the spot where something had vanished in the woods. "What are you?" he said into the woods.

As two officers reached the car, Jake heard the predator flee into the woods. Steve Crandall approached, "Peterson? What is it?"

"I'm not sure, but I think it's gone."

"Was it our victim?" he asked.

"I don't think so."

"Then what was it?" Steve said looking around uncertainly.

"I'm not sure. Something. Maybe a wild animal of some kind."

They looked into the woods trying to see anything. Off to their left, something began running away, crashing through the undergrowth. Jake watched the dark shadow as it climbed up the embankment away from them.

As it reached the top, it turned and looked back at Jake. Its red eyes were illuminated in the dark woods like the eyes of an animal caught in the light. Jake gasped in surprise.

"What? Do you see something?" Steve said looking in the direction Jake was looking at, but saw nothing.

"It's gone," he said. He was shaken and knew it. Jake leaned back against his truck and tried to calm his nerves.

"What do you think it was?"

"A wild dog of some kind. I think there were two," he turned and pointed down the driveway. "Over there is where I saw it first, but then there was growling behind me, so I swung around. When I yelled, I think I scared them off."

Jake was still searching for sight of the creatures, but knew they were gone. He looked at Steve and shrugged and gave him a half smile, "I better get over to the church. I've got to figure out what's next."

Jake opened the truck door and began to get inside. "Wait a minute," Steve said. "What about the case?"

Jake looked at him in surprise. "The case?" Jake shook his head. "I already told the Captain that I'm not getting involved. You should probably tell the searchers to be careful with that animal wandering around." Jake looked back up the hill toward where he saw the creature disappear. He thought he could make out a shape up there and felt his fear begin to return.

"My last day is Friday. The department could use your help with these cases. I heard the captain talking to Riley and Burgess about it. Bennett thinks you can't get past Riley."

"It doesn't have anything to do with Meg. I've got to run a church and I don't know where to begin."

"Hey, it doesn't matter to me. I'm leaving remember?"

"I really have to go," Jake said getting in his truck. Steve shook his head with a knowing smile and walked back to the house.

As Jake started his truck, he couldn't help looking back up at the hill. Everything looked fine, but he could sense something out there. He shuddered and put the truck in reverse and almost backed into a tree. He slowly backed the truck up until he was near the tree where the first creature had been. There was nothing there now. Jake backed his truck out onto the deserted road and drove to the church.

CHAPTER 5

Jake stopped at the church to call Mrs. Baxter, the church secretary, and a few of the elders. They started a prayer chain for Walt's quick recovery. When he told Mrs. Baxter that he really needed to get a few hours of sleep, she disapproved and told him so. Jake was surprised because he thought of her as such a mild-tempered person. But when it came to the administration of the church, she was serious that things would stay in order while Pastor Walt was ill.

Mrs. Baxter had a list of responsibilities that Jake needed to cover and a schedule for the week. Jake understood that he would need to do the counseling, but thought that Mrs. Baxter could make sure the announcements were okay for the bulletin. He could barely get a word in as she told him what she thought of his idea. As she talked, he sat looking at a picture of her and her husband on their last anniversary that sat on her desk. Jake remembered her wearing the same lavender dress to church with its tiny dark purple flowers.

Corinne Baxter was a beautiful woman with long silver hair she worn pined up in a neat bun. Her husband, Jerry, was just as small and waif like as she was. They both had the same brown eyes. They looked happy in the picture. Finally, after hearing details about the upcoming pot luck supper, Jake promised to be back at the church right after her lunch break. As he drove home, he imagined her five foot tiny frame all worked up over the pot luck supper planned for Saturday night and had a good laugh.

Now, Jake sat in the truck in front of his little A-Frame house that was across the road from the lake. The long night caught up with him and he was exhausted. Jake looked at the stacks of lumber that were sitting next to the side deck as he climbed out of the truck. He sighed knowing that the work he had planned for the fall would be delayed.

He had wanted to buy a house just like this one when he was dating Meg with the hopes that they would live in it together one day. But Meg never wanted a little house in the country. Jake couldn't believe when he came back to town that the little house he dreamed of had been for sale. It was rustic with its opened rooms, exposed oak beams, and hardwood floors. Jake had already starting fixing it up with the dream of breathing life into the old camp house again. He found a lot of his furnishing at an antique auction in Vermont.

Jake went up the back deck in through the kitchen door. He tossed his keys on top of the junk that had accumulated on his dishwasher. Getting a cold soda from the refrigerator, Jake looked out into the living room to see his German Shepherd sprawled out on the couch sound asleep. He twisted off the cap of the soda and took a long swallow.

"Hey, Buddy, some watch dog you turned out to be." Buddy never moved and Jake laughed quietly. He really wanted to just go to bed, but he was bothered by some of the things Meg had said to him. Jake went upstairs to his small office.

Jake sat down at the computer terminal and turned it on. While he waited for the computer, his saw his Bible that he had left there the day before. He picked it up and flipped through it to the book of Psalms where he knew he would find strength for the upcoming days. But Jake couldn't concentrate as his mind drifted back to the Stanwicks and the old case he had worked on. Finally, Jake sighed and decided to get some sleep. It had been a long night and he had to get to the church to figure a few things out. Taking a few minutes, he looked at his own e-mail inbox and found that he had a few messages waiting for him. He drank the rest of his soda, read the e-mail messages, and then shut down the computer.

Jake walked down the narrow hall between the rooms and the balcony that overlooked the living room. He threw his clothes at the hamper and half missed. He fell into his bed and pulled the sheet up. An hour later, Buddy lay next to Jake whimpering looking toward the window as Jake slept.

CHAPTER 6

Sam Craig shifted his backpack and he began climbing the embankment. He knew he was going to hear it from his mother when he walked in the door, so he purposely walked slowly. Ted Petrie was a jerk and Sam would show him. Sam kicked a rock and it bounced a few times and rolled down the embankment. Everybody thought Ted was so great. At eleven, Ted already seemed destined to be the star quarterback on the high school team. Athletic, a great student and all the girls thought he was so cute. Sam made a face as he thought how he heard Melinda Yates giggling with the other sixth grade girls. Yeah, Melinda really liked Ted. Sam might as well forget about asking her to their first dance.

Until school started, Sam thought that he had a "special" friendship with Melinda. That was until that first day, when the new kid, Ted Petrie, came to town and wrecked everything for Sam. Until school started, he had been looking forward to going to middle school and having Mrs. Waters for his teacher. His older sister, Karen, had Mrs. Waters. Karen told him how great she was, but so far, all she did was embarrass Sam in front of the whole class. But it was really Melinda that got to Sam.

Sam stopped in front of the railroad tracks and looked down it both ways. He knew he should be walking along Main Street instead of cutting through the woods. But so what, he was already in hot water with his mother. He shrugged and stepped over the rail and started walking down the middle of the tracks. Right about now, he couldn't get into any more trouble with his folks. His thoughts drifted back to the lunchroom where his best friend, Johnny Mendoza, pointed out Melinda sitting next to Ted. Melinda always sat at their table. Melinda, Sam, Johnny, and Carolyn, Melinda's best friend, sat together at lunch since third grade. Now, Melinda and Carolyn sat on either side of Ted talking and laughing. Sam felt himself getting mad all over again.

Sam wanted this new kid to know this was his school, Melinda was his girl, and he wasn't going to let this new kid come in and take over. Melinda. Her dark brown eyes were an opened book when she talked. Sam found himself lost in those eyes. She had the most beautiful long hair that she always wears loose with bangs, always a bit too long. Sam knew in his heart he'd never love anyone like Melinda. He hoped one day she'd feel the same about him. That was until Sam saw Melinda looking at Ted the way she did at Mr. Carlson in fourth grade. He wished with all his heart that Melinda would look at him like that, just once. But she always treated him like her buddy.

Sam knew he couldn't compete with Ted. He was just too ordinary. Sam was just an average kid, dirty brown hair, braces, and average grades. Nobody paid him any special attention, he was just another kid. Until school started and Ted came. Now he was always in trouble with his teacher and even his friends were leery about him. Sam was only trying to be better than Ted, but he kept making a fool out of himself. But today took the cake. Melinda was holding hands with Ted!! Sam couldn't stand it anymore. He was tired of being in Ted's shadow, and it was only October.

While Sam ate his lunch, he watched them hardly paying attention to Johnny who was talking about the neat science project he was going to create. He was watching every move that Ted made on his girl. He didn't really plan it too well, it just happened. When Ted and Melinda got up to throw out their garbage, they had to walk right past Sam. That's when Sam decided to make a fool out of Ted. Carolyn and Melinda passed by him first and then he stuck his foot out into the aisle. Stupid move since Ted was so athletic. But Sam didn't think it through. Ted tripped, but caught himself. The half empty carton of milk tittered and Ted couldn't catch it since he was off balance. Sam didn't see it coming and the milk landed upside down in his lap.

Sam jumped up and the huge milk puddle quickly soaked into his pants. Some eighth graders at the next table burst out laughing. Milk ran down Sam's pant legs. He was humiliated, and it was Ted's fault again. He took a swing at Ted and managed to knock the lunch tray out of Ted's hands. The tray sprayed food all over Melinda who had turned back to see what was going on. Sam froze as Melinda looked at him with dark brown eyes filling with tears. She fled for the girl's room with Carolyn at her heels.

Sam was still mad and grabbed at Ted intending to pulverize him. But Ted was too quick and hit him first, landing a solid punch in Sam's gut.

Unfortunately for Sam, Mrs. Waters had seen the whole incident and was headed their way. Sam's return punch hit Mrs. Waters right in her stomach. Mr. Brannon, the vice principal, called his mother while he sat in front of his huge mahogany desk. Sam wondered if the desk was so big just to make kids feel really small. Mr. Brannon coached high school track and was already on a friendly basis with Ted. Sam knew he was sunk.

His anger turned to cold fear while he listened to Mr. Brannon tell his mother what happened. His father would kill him when he got home from work. He had been warned about his behavior problems. This would be the end of everything for a very long while. He knew that when he got home that his video games would already be gone, along with his bike, and whatever else his mother could find in his room to hold for ransom. But the week's suspension from school for hitting a teacher, he'd be lucky if he weren't grounded until Christmas!

Sam couldn't help but think about Melinda and how she ran out in tears. He never even saw her again. He was sent to Mr. Brannon's office and stayed there until after the buses left. Sam normally walked home from school anyway, so Mr. Brannon made sure he stayed put until the school was just about empty.

Sam stopped on the tracks. It was getting late and dusk was slowly seeping in. The woods surrounding the tracks seemed even darker. Sam felt uncomfortable and glanced around him. He looked back down the tracks to the overpass where he climbed up and couldn't see it. The path that cut back over to his street was still a way up on the right. He knew that the woods would be dark by the time he got to the path. Sam stood for a minute undecided. Shrugging, he walked toward the path. If he got lost in the woods, maybe they'd all feel sorry they were so mean to him.

Sam thought he saw something in the woods. The shadows seemed to move next to him. Sam started walking faster and so did the shadow. A low growling started and Sam felt a hard knot of fear in his stomach. He ran down the tracks toward the path. The path was on the right and Sam jumped off the tracks and ran toward it. He heard the animal behind him. Sam screamed as he collided with a man in the middle of the path.

"Whoa, kid," the man started. Sam was screaming and hitting at the man. The man grabbed him and held on while Sam continued to struggle. "Calm down, kid. I'm not going to hurt you."

24

The voice broke through Sam's fears and he began to relax. "That's better. Something after you or do you just pummel every person you see in the woods."

Sam pulled out of the man's grasp and tried to catch his breath. He took big gulps of air and glanced back over his shoulder. "Kid, is something out there?"

Sam nodded still looking around. Still breathing hard, Sam said, "Yeah, something was chasing me and it growled."

"Well, if a wild animal was chasing you, it wouldn't have stopped just because you ran into me."

"You sure? You're an adult, sometimes, adults make things go away."

"I'm sure kid. Wild animals would keep coming regardless of whether or not I was an adult. You live around here?"

Sam looked up at the man. Dressed all in black, the stranger was handsome with an olive complexion, black wavy hair and dark eyes. In the growing dusk, it was hard for Sam to really see the man, but he knew he didn't know him.

"Yeah. Down this path to Dunning," Sam said.

"That's quite a ways this late in the day. You got a name kid?"

"Sam."

"Well, Sam. It's nice to meet you. I'm Trevor." Trevor stuck his hand out and Sam shook it.

There was a rustling in the woods and Sam stepped closer to Trevor. "What is that?" he whispered.

Trevor looked toward the noise and smiled. "That's just my dog. Maybe he's what scared you on the tracks."

"If he's your dog, why doesn't he come out?"

"You wouldn't like that. He's kind of mean, but as long as you're with me or he knows you're my friend, he won't hurt you. Okay, Sam?"

Sam glanced back at the big shape in the woods near the path and then glanced up at Trevor. "Are we friends? I don't know you." Sam got a weird feeling from Trevor and his voice trembled.

"What do you think, Sam?" Trevor put his hand on Sam's shoulder. "Don't you want to be my friend?" From the darkness, the dog growled and it sent fear racing through Sam. He looked back over at the woods and saw glowing red eyes looking back at him.

"Yeah, Trevor. I want to be your friend." Sam couldn't control his fear and he pressed himself close to Trevor. Trevor looked down at Sam and put his arm protectively around his shoulders. He said something foreign to the animal and it turned and ran into the woods.

"What did you say to him?" Sam whispered.

"It's alright. I told him you were my friend. He won't bother you unless you betray that friendship. Now, why don't I walk you home? After all, he has a sister that is just as mean tempered as him."

Sam nodded and glanced around him at the woods again. As they walked up the path toward Dunning Street, the dark animals followed behind them in the woods. The woods seemed to close in on Sam, but with Trevor's arm resting on his shoulder he felt safer. Once they reached the lighted street, Trevor took his arm away.

"Do you live around here?" Sam asked feeling safer now that he was close to home.

"I came for the track season and decided to stay. There are a lot of nice people here." Trevor looked down smiling. Sam turned down his road and could see his front porch light on and his mother standing in the doorway.

"That's my house right down there. My mom might not like it that you're with me. I got in trouble at school and she's not going to be in a good mood."

"Don't worry about your mother. I'll talk to her. I'd rather not leave you alone with my dogs loose out there." Trevor gestured toward the woods sending a chill down Sam's spine. "It will be alright. I promise, after all you are my friend."

Sam looked up at Trevor and saw the smile and nodded. "I guess I can't get into any more trouble anyway. I punched my teacher today."

Trevor laughed. "You're kidding, aren't you?"

Sam sadly shook his head. "Nope. I did it. And the principal called my mom."

They walked toward the house in silence. Trevor with an amused smile on his face knowing he picked the right kid. When Clara Craig saw her son walking up the darkening road with a strange man, she rushed out the door and practically ran down the street toward them. The dark creatures turned their attention toward the woman, but waited for a sign from their master.

Clara started yelling at Sam before she reached him. Sam sighed and looked at Trevor. "Where have you been? School's been out for hours. I've been worried sick. And who is this?" Clara looked right into Trevor's eyes and took a sharp intake of her breath. The dark creatures tensed in the woods. Trevor stuck his hand out.

"I'm Trevor Grant. We are neighbors. I just live down the road a few houses."

Clara looked at the hand and slipped her small hand into his. "Clara Craig. Sam's mother. You're the one that moved into the old house?"

"It is a pleasure to meet you Mrs. Craig. And yes, that would be me." He turned her hand over and kissed it. The kiss sent a tingling feeling up Clara's arm and caused her heart to beat faster. She was thankful for the gloom to hide her blushed cheeks. She pulled her hand out of Trevor's and turned her attention to Sam.

"Dinner's waiting and so is your father. I'm sorry Mr. Grant, but it's late and I've been very worried about my son."

"I understand. I was walking him home to be sure he got home safely." Clara seemed flustered and unsure of herself. "Um… Do you need to eat?"

"Thank you for the kind offer, but I have plans this evening for dinner. It was a pleasure meeting you and Sam and I hope to get to know you better. Perhaps one evening next week, you and your family will join me at my home for dinner."

"Of course. Give me a call. We are in the phone book. Come on Sam, your father is waiting."

Trevor nodded his head and watched as Clara began to berate Sam again as they walked toward the house. Yes. He made the right choice in choosing Sam. He stood on the side of the road as they closed the door to their house and the porch light went off. One of the creatures came and sat at his feet and whimpered. Trevor dropped his hand on the creature's large head and stroked the thick fur. Soon, very soon.

CHAPTER 7

Dinner was a nightmare for Sam. Karen ate as quickly as she could and disappeared to her room. The blaring from her radio told Sam that she didn't want to hear anything anymore. Between being yelled at for what happened at school and being yelled at for walking home with a stranger, he found himself grounded until after Halloween. Not that it mattered, since all of his friends were more interested in Ted than him now. Clara kept going between nagging and crying until finally she went to her room with a headache. Her pale freckled face was splotched with red from her crying. She took several sleeping pills that she had hidden in her bathroom that she needed badly.

Sam sat picking at the cold pork chops thinking about Trevor and the weird feeling he had when he walked home with him. Stanley Craig began to stack the dirty dishes knowing his wife would be sleeping in less than an hour. He had a nagging headache too. Sam looked just like Stanley did when he was his age, but Stanley didn't have the problems that his son had. Stanley was a great student, but just ordinary looking like Sam. The same dirty brown hair and brown eyes. The same round face with a spattering of freckles. Karen looked just like Clara with the red hair, light green eyes and pale skin. And much to Stanley's chagrin, the same fiery temper.

Stanley watched as Sam pushed the peas around on his plate and felt aggravated again. Finally he sat back down sighing. Sam looked at his father, "Dad, can I ask you something?"

"I think I've had all I can take for one night, Sam," he said as he dropped his head down into his hands.

"It's nothing about the trouble I'm in. I just have a question about animals." Stanley looked up curious. "What makes an animal's eyes red in the dark?"

"Like when they get caught in light?"

Sam looked back at the plate and pushed the peas around some more. "Well, something like that, but just in the dark. Why would an animal's eyes glow red?"

"They won't. Their eyes only look red when they reflect light."

"I saw an animal in the woods tonight that's eyes were glowing red and it wasn't in the light. What kind of animal would do that?"

"Sam look at me." Sam looked up at his father. "Are you playing a game with me?"

"No, sir." Stanley looked closely at his son to see if he was lying. "Dad, I saw something in the woods tonight that really scared me. It growled and its eyes glowed red. I couldn't really see it because it stayed in the woods and it was dark. If I hadn't run into Trevor, I think it would have gotten me."

Sam's eyes filled up with tears. The long day had finally gotten to him and the fear of what he encountered in the darkness terrified him. He tried to hold back the tears, but they slid down his cheeks anyway.

"I don't know. It could have been some kind of a wild animal, like a wolf or a bear. What did this Trevor say?"

"Trevor said," Sam sucked in his breath as he tried to stop crying. He thought about what Trevor told him about betraying his friendship and what his dogs would do. But he was scared. He started again, "He said that an adult couldn't make a wild animal go away. He didn't think it was a wild animal."

"What did he think it was?"

Sam shrugged and glanced at his father. His tears had stopped, but he waited for an answer. "Well, I don't know what to tell you, Sam. If Trevor didn't see it and you didn't see it, I can't tell you what it is. An animal's eyes won't glow without light reflecting in them. And if there is something out in the woods, you better stick close to home until I've had a chance to look around. That shouldn't be a problem since you're grounded for now anyway. Why don't you help me clean this mess up?"

Sam nodded and began helping his father in silence. Stanley watched Sam while he helped feeling uneasy. It wasn't like Sam to make up a story just to get out of trouble and he wouldn't just cry unless he really was scared. When they finished, Sam went off to his room to begin his grounding and Stanley went into his office. It was a small bedroom on the first floor that Stanley had converted into an office. He had plans of setting up a private accounting practice and doing taxes for his neighbors. But when he showed the office to

Clara and told of his plan, she laughed it off as a joke. So, now it just was a room that Stanley escaped to when he came home from work. He turned on his computer and began an Internet search on wild animals found in the Northeast.

Sam sat on the end of his bed looking forlornly at the empty space in the corner where his TV and video games had sat until around 2 o'clock that afternoon. Clara had even taken his army men that he hadn't played with in over two years. He could hear the music from Karen's room drift down the hall from her room. It was a lot quieter since his mother had fled to her room, so he couldn't tell what song it was. It wouldn't matter in about another hour. Karen would shut off the music before she went to sleep.

Sam got off the bed and looked under it. Well, his mother hadn't been as thorough as usual. He found a few comic books that had found their way under the bed and pulled them out. Although he wasn't a huge Spiderman fan, it would help to pass some of the night away. Sam climbed back on the bed and propped up his pillow against the wall and leaned back against it. He had already read the comic book before, but it was something to do.

As he reached over onto his desk to turn on the lamp, he glanced out the window. He sucked in his breath as he saw two red glowing eyes looking up at him in the darkness. He reached out and pulled the blind down to block out the sight, but knew that the dark creature from the woods was watching him. Sam got up and shut the lights off in his room and went back to the window. Carefully peeking through a crack in the blinds, he could still see the eyes outside. He wanted to run downstairs and tell his father, but knew that somehow the creature would know. Sam sank down onto the bed and curled up into a ball wishing it were morning. It was a long time before he drifted off to sleep.

CHAPTER 8

Sam sat at the table eating cold cereal that had gotten soggy. Clara sat at the other end nursing a cup of coffee. She needed to get herself pulled together since she had to be at her job at the bank in less than an hour. She glared at Sam blaming him for her headache.

"Just so you know, this isn't a vacation from school. You will be expected to accomplish something so I know what you're up to when I'm at work," Clara said and Sam sunk lower in the chair. Sam had sat up until 2 in the morning watching the creature watch the house. He fell into an exhausted sleep and awoke to his mother banging on his door just before she got into the shower.

"There is a list on the dishwasher and that is just the beginning of what your father and I came up with," she continued. "You want to make a fool out of yourself and embarrass your family. You'll pay one way or another." She finished the last of her coffee and walked to the dishwasher. She glanced at the list and added cleaning up the kitchen to the bottom of it. "And I'm going to call you every hour and make sure you answer the phone. Do you understand me, young man?"

"Yeah," she heard him softly answer.

"What? I didn't hear you."

"Yes," he said louder. Satisfied, Clara walked out the back door heading toward her car. She would need to stop at the convenient store for a large coffee if she was going to make it to lunchtime.

Sam continued swirling the cereal around in the bowl. Alone in the house, he could almost hear the silence. With a sigh, he got up and brought his bowl to the sink. He picked up the list and began to read the various jobs that he had been assigned to complete. On top of that, the principal said that Johnny would be bringing him homework every day. Sam dumped the rest of his cereal down the disposal and rinsed his bowl out. He rinsed the breakfast dishes and put them in the dishwasher, then turned it on. He took the leftover coffee from the coffeepot and poured it into a coffee cup. Taking a sip of the lukewarm coffee, he grimaced.

Sam went back to the table and dumped a bunch of sugar in the cup and stirred it. He took another sip and found it wasn't as bad. He went back and got the list and sat down to drink the coffee. If it worked for his mother, maybe it would work for him too. The list was huge and Sam couldn't see how he'd be able to get it all done in one week, let alone one day. He dropped the list on the table and took his coffee into the living room. He put on the TV and sat drinking the coffee while flipping through the channels. Sam realized at that time of the morning, nothing would be on that interested him. He watched a newscaster talking to a couple about their vacation and then listened to the weather report. Clear and unseasonably warm for the next five days. Great, Sam moaned. No sign of rain to put off cleaning out the garage and scraping the side of the house.

Feeling revived from the coffee, Sam decided to get started with the list. Maybe his parents will give him a break if he got a lot done today. "Fat chance," he said to no one as he rinsed out the coffee cup and put it back in the cupboard. No sense making more trouble for himself.

Sam went outside and started picking up the lawn. The lawn chairs which had been deserted on Labor Day weekend still sat out in the middle of the lawn with grass grown up to the seats. His father wasn't big about doing yard work, but with Sam's free labor, it seemed time to clean up. Sam folded the chairs and put them inside the garage. He took down the volleyball net, gathered the balls and Frisbees and put them near the chairs.

Sam pulled the walk behind lawn mower out of the garage and opened the gas tank. He found a half full gas can in the garage and put more gas in the mower. He easily started the mower and began the trips around the yard. An hour later, the back yard was mowed and Sam wandered back into the house for a drink. He found the message light on the answering machine blinking.

Sam moaned in the silent house. He glanced up at the clock realizing he was supposed to answer the phone when his mother called. As if on cue, the phone rang.

"Where have you been?" his mother demanded.

Sam winced at her tone. "I was outside mowing the lawn. I didn't hear the phone ring."

"I told you I was going to call. I was about to come home. Make sure you answer the phone next time. What have you gotten done?"

Sam glanced around. "I cleaned up the kitchen and the back yard. Then I mowed the lawn."

"Well, at least you accomplished something. I'll call back in an hour. Answer the phone. Do you hear me?"

"Yes." Before she could say anymore, Sam hung up. Sam went to the refrigerator and pulled out a bottle of Pepsi. He put the cold bottle against the side of his face and he walked to the cupboard to get a glass. He poured himself a glass of soda and the phone rang again.

"Leave me alone!" Sam yelled at the phone. But it rang again. He couldn't keep the disgust out of his voice as he answered the phone.

"Hello to you too, scumbag." Johnny said.

"Hey, I thought you were my mother again."

"Tough, man. I'm glad I'm not you."

"I'm glad I'm not you either." Sam jumped up on the counter next to his glass and leaned back against the cupboard. "So, what's new?"

"You are *the* talk of the town. Man, hitting a teacher."

"Yeah, well, see where it landed me. Seven days of solitary confinement, with hard labor."

"Ted and Melinda are going out now." Sam felt like Johnny just punched him in the stomach. When he didn't say anything, Johnny went on. "They were walking around this morning holding hands. Carolyn told me that Ted walked Melinda home yesterday and he felt bad about what happened in the cafeteria with you. Then he just asked if she wanted to go out and she said yes. Oh, no. It's Mr. Fielding, I need to go. I'll see you after school."

Sam found he couldn't breathe. It was like he was in a dream. He put the phone down and just sat for a few minutes trying to understand what Johnny said. It was his fault. Because of the fight, Ted asked Melinda out. It all was because of Ted that this happened and now he would be out of school and couldn't make it right with Melinda for a week. Too late to salvage anything. The anger built up and Sam ran out of the house. He looked at the lawn mower waiting for him to finish the front lawn. He knew his mother would be calling back in less than an hour.

Sam took off toward the woods, his haven from all the bad stuff. He found the caves two years ago when he was hiding out from one of his mother's bad times. In those days, she was only mean and moody when his father was out of town. One day, trying to escape her berating Sam for his father's failings, Sam found the caves.

Sam ran for the safety of the dark cool caves. He could stay there for days because he had hidden a flashlight, some canned foods, and some of the camping stuff that his father had from college in the small cave. Maybe they'd all feel sorry they were so mean to him if he just disappeared like that lady that was on the news a few weeks ago.

It took Sam fifteen minutes to get to the caves. There were several caves that lined the mountain and Sam liked the ones that were up higher. He didn't mind that he had to climb up to them since that meant anything trying to get him would have to climb up the rocks too. He climbed to the safety of his cave. Inside the small cave, Sam found the stuff he had left there two months before. Hidden in a small alcove behind a big rock, Sam had put a large black garbage bag full of stuff. He was happy to see it undisturbed. The sleeping bag was dry and the flashlight still worked. Sam took the food out and realized he didn't have as much food as he thought.

Sam pulled a notebook out of the bag that had a pen stuck in the spiral and wrote down a few things he didn't want to forget from the house. He stuck everything back in the bag and went back to the house. The phone was ringing as he got to the kitchen door. He quickly answered it.

"Glad you answered it this time. What else have you gotten done?" Clara began.

Sam glanced at the list that was on the table. "I'm working on the garage."

"Good. Don't forget if you eat lunch to clean up after yourself. I don't want to come home to a bunch of dirty dishes."

"Sure, Mom. Better get going. I've got a lot to do."

Clara felt unsettled. "You alright, Sam?"

"Sure. Just want to get this all done. Bye." He hung up quickly and went to the refrigerator. Pulling out a loaf of bread, Sam made himself ten peanut butter and jelly sandwiches. He found a box of Ritz Crackers and put them with the sandwiches. He went up to his room and grabbed some long sleeved shirts and pants and put them in his duffel bag. He put some comic books and his Walkman in the bag on top of his clothes. He went back to the kitchen and took a large garbage bag and put the sandwiches, crackers, a few cans of soda, and a few other snacks into the bag. He stuffed his winter coat on top of it. He went to the junk drawer and found some extra batteries and put them in the duffel bag with his clothes. He looked around the kitchen to see if there was anything else that he could use and then left.

Sam walked back through the woods toward the caves. The trip back with all the stuff took him longer than before, but it didn't matter. His mother wouldn't really come back to the house to check on him and his father wouldn't be home until really late. It took two trips up to his cave to get all the stuff up there. Sam took everything out of the bags and arranged the cave as if it was a bedroom. He kept the sandwiches wrapped up in the garbage bag to keep the bugs out. On a ledge he set up the cans of soda, canned foods, extra batteries, and his comic books. He decided to keep his clothes in the duffel bag since he didn't want bugs in them either. After he arranged his stuff, he settled down with the Walkman and a comic book.

CHAPTER 9

Jake drove the back roads of Granelle toward Little T's Trailer Park. Between yesterday afternoon and this morning, he found it was going to be difficult to keep up with Mrs. Baxter. The paperwork alone seemed daunting to Jake and then the counseling. One couple made it clear that Jake wouldn't be counseling them in their marital problems. After all, what did a single young man know about marital problems? Although it was a temporary situation, the wife told Mrs. Baxter that perhaps the Presbyterian minister could counsel them and they would need to attend that church in the interim.

Millie had called to tell them that Pastor Walt's open heart surgery was successful and that he would be in the hospital for several more days. So it fell on Jake to write the annual appeal letter because Mrs. Baxter said it had to be done so that it could go to the printer. If it was late, they would never get it mailed out on time, and the missionaries the church supported wouldn't have their Christmas gifts for the children.

Jake was still trying to figure out how to write the annual appeal letter when he got a call from Jessie Buchanan who was in one of the never-ending battles with her husband. Mrs. Baxter had made it clear that she thought it was inappropriate for Jake to go to the trailer park, after all, he was acting in the role as senior pastor now. But Jake had been working with the Buchanan's since he came back to Granelle. Having arrested Clyde numerous times for being drunk, Jessie felt he was the one person who could help save her husband.

But Jake knew it was really because he needed the break, and much to the disapproval of Mrs. Baxter, chose to go to the trailer to help sort out the fight. Of course, he had to promise to be back quickly so that he could give Mrs. Baxter the name of his sermon for Sunday. It was Friday and the name had to be in the bulletin so she could get it done and copied. The problem was that Jake didn't even know what to talk about yet.

On top of that, Jake found his thoughts returning again and again to the Stanwicks. It was bothering Jake and he knew it was his pride. He wasn't a cop anymore and he struggled with his place being involved as a minister. Once George's parents arrived, they made it clear that Jake didn't need to come over and neither did anyone else from the church. George, feeling lost without Kathy, let his mother take over the house.

The radio played some music in the background, and as he approached the trailer park, Jake leaned over and turned the radio off. As he turned in to the park, Jake noticed a police cruiser already in front of the trailer. The truck pulled up in front of the trailer and Jake could hear the shouting. He walked up the dilapidated porch and knocked on the door. The shouting just got louder. Jake knocked again on the door. Something crashed inside and Jake opened the door. A lamp was lying in the middle of the floor.

Greg Matthews was standing between them trying to calm them down. When Clyde saw Jake he said, "She's crazy Pastor Jake. I'm not even drunk."

"Yes you are…you always are," Jessie Buchanan shouted back. She was holding a frying pan and stepped toward Clyde threatening him. Clyde held up his hands in defense.

"Get that thing away from her," he whined to Greg. Greg was a young officer who had been hired to replace Steve Crandall. He looked too young to be a cop even with the uniform on. He wore his hair in a short crew cut and Jake saw the lack of experience in his innocent blue eyes.

Jake stepped into the room and took charge. "Okay, let's just talk about this. Jessie give the officer the frying pan and go with him into the kitchen." Jake stepped over toward Clyde.

"Oh sure, take his side. You men always stick together, don't you?" Jessie shouted turning her attention to Jake.

"Jessie, you know me better than that. I don't take sides. I'm just trying to get you two to stop fighting so much. All this yelling disturbs your neighbors."

"I don't care about them."

"Jessie, why don't you come with me into the other room and tell me all about it," Greg said intervening and he grabbed her arm. She jerked away and swung the frying pan hitting Greg in the arm. Jake grabbed her from behind restraining her. Greg was able to get the frying pan out of her hand.

"Ah, Jessie, why'd you go and do that," Clyde whined. "You just hit a cop."

"I don't care," she said still screaming.

"I'm going to have to take you in," Greg said trying to take over again. "That's assault. All I wanted you to do was to go in the kitchen and talk to me so we could figure out what was going on." She began crying as Greg put the handcuffs on her.

"She didn't mean it," Clyde said. "Why you taking her in? Jake never did."

Greg looked at Jake uncertain. Jake shrugged, "I'm their minister, but I used to be on the force."

"Oh, you didn't arrest them for assaulting you?" he asked looking at Jake wide eyed. Jessie was still crying but looked at Jake for help.

"Officer, just take her to the car and radio for backup. I'll stay here until Det. Riley gets here. You'll need a woman escort to take her in," Jake replied knowing that if he backed the Buchanans, Greg would have no authority in the town.

Greg just nodded and led Jessie outside. She cried louder as she sunk down in the backseat of the police cruiser. As Greg went to close the door, Jake stopped him and knelt down beside her. Greg opened the front door and radioed the dispatcher.

"What's going on Jess? It's not like you to be hitting people," Jake said quietly.

"He's cheating on me." Jessie said as she continued to cry.

"How do you know that?"

"I saw them. All the times I forgave him for coming home drunk, for hitting me, for bailing him out for drunk driving, and he cheats on me. Don't let them bring me to jail, Pastor Jake. You know I'm a good person."

"I'm sorry, Jessie. You can't hit an officer and get away with it. It's the same thing I always told you about Clyde. There is never a reason to hit someone."

"What's going to happen to me now?"

"When Det. Riley gets here, she'll read you your rights and then you'll go down to the station where you will be booked. Then you can call a lawyer who will help you. Same thing that Clyde had to go through when he was arrested for drunk driving."

Jessie shook her head and sat there for a few minutes. "Pastor Jake when I get that phone call, can I call anyone I want?"

"Sure you can, but don't you want to call your lawyer?"

"No, I want to call my nephew."

"Is he a lawyer?"

"Nope. He's a preacher. He's got a little church over in Ballston Lake. Maybe you're right and it's time to let God help me with my problems." Jessie looked up at Jake. Her face was tear stained and wet. "You think God does care about me?"

"Jessie I know that God cares. I'll be praying for you."

Greg came over to them. "I really should close the door until Officer Riley gets here."

"Okay," Jake said standing. "I'll talk to Clyde."

Jake went to the porch where Clyde was standing watching. As he walked up the steps, he glanced at the trailer next door. He waved at the partial opened blinds that quickly snapped shut.

"So, do you know why she got so mad tonight?" Jake asked when he got to the top of the porch.

"No, she wouldn't tell me what was going on. I figured she thought I was drunk again."

"She didn't?" Jake said turning toward Clyde. "She was threatening you with a frying pan and didn't tell you that she caught you cheating on her?"

"Cheating?" Clyde looked sheepishly. "I didn't cheat."

"Well, that's between you and your wife. All we know is that you two were fighting again and this time it's Jessie who's going to jail. Clyde, you know the truth, not me."

"Pastor Jake, it didn't mean nothing. It was just a fling. Why'd she get so mad?"

Jake put his hand on Clyde's shoulder, "She got so mad because she loves you. You betrayed her by cheating on her."

"But everyone fools around from time to time."

"No, they don't Clyde. The Bible is clear about adultery. You claim to have asked the Lord into your life and that means a changed life."

"Now don't start preaching at me. I'm still a sinner you know."

Jake heard a car pull up and looked to see Meg getting out of a car. Jake watched her go over to Greg. "Officer, is this Jessie?" he heard her ask.

"Yes, you'll need to search her and read her her rights. Should I get a statement from her husband?"

"No, I'll do it. She hit you, right?"

"Yes, and Jake saw it too."

Meg looked over and saw Jake standing with Clyde. Jake waved lamely at her surprised look. She walked over and asked tersely, "What are you doing here?"

"Jessie called me when they started fighting. I'm their minster too."

"You just keep showing up all over the place. I don't recall seeing Pastor Ryerson this much."

"Well, I'm just trying to be here for the people."

"Then, can you wait inside while I do my job, Reverend. I'll need to take a statement from you," she said sarcastically.

"Sure," Jake said and stepped inside the trailer with Clyde. Jake hoped to talk to him some more, but Clyde went down the hall.

Meg came into the trailer a few minutes later. "I need to bring her in. Can you both come to the station so we can get your statements?"

Jake looked uncomfortable, "To the station? Can't you take it here?"

"No. Greg needs to leave on another call and I can't just leave Jessie sitting in the back of the car. If you come down to the station, Pete can take your statements. Is that a problem?"

"No, I guess not," Jake said resigned.

"What's wrong?" Meg asked with a little concern.

"I just haven't been to the station since I left to go to seminary. Just a little strange," he shrugged. "Well, let's just get this over with."

CHAPTER 10

Jake sat reading the statement that was typed for his signature. He didn't understand why everyone thought this was so amusing. Pete typed slow and joked the whole time. To them it was just another domestic dispute, but to Jake it was a person he was just learning to care about. It bothered him that Jessie was in lock-up waiting to be processed to have bail set. Meg sat down in the chair next to him as Jake tried to ignore her. She pushed a file on top of the paper he was reading.

"I guess we can't keep avoiding this," Meg said. "Bennett wants you to read the lab reports on the Stanwick case."

"I already told Reggie I wasn't going to work for the police department." Jake picked up her folder and held it out for her. "I've got to get back to the church."

"Look, I don't like this any better than you do. This is my case and I've worked hard to prove myself to Bennett after you left. But he thinks we need your opinion. So just read it."

"What would Reggie do if I hadn't come back to Granelle? I don't have time for this."

"If it was up to me, I wouldn't even want you anywhere near this case. I think it's connected and if it is, that means you screwed up. But that's not the way the Captain sees it. He thinks you're the golden boy. So take the file, read it, and then call me. Better yet, call Bennett, he cares about your opinion."

She stood and walked away leaving Jake holding the file out to no one. He put the file down on the side of the cluttered desk. He heard a chuckle and looked over at Pete who had been watching the exchange.

"Peterson, what brings you out here?"

Jake looked up at Reggie smiling down at him, "Just had to sign a witness statement," Jake replied leaning back in the chair.

"Well while you're here, we can use your expertise."

"Reggie, I can't help you. I've got to get over to the church."

"Tell you what, you pray about it and let me know if you feel like the Big Boss would let you help us. Okay?"

"Reggie, that's not fair."

"I'm serious. Pray about it and then call me. Okay?" Reggie said. He left Jake and went back into his office and closed the door.

Jake looked around the squad room. It was empty at this time of the day, but the shift change would be coming in the next hour. He glanced at the folder that Meg left and pulled it in front of him. He thought about Douglas Angelos. Angelos was one of the track people. He cleaned up after the horses and followed them from track to track. He was a loser that was trying to win it big at the track.

Angelos was a big guy, six-five, and well over 300 lbs, with greasy black hair that he combed straight back. He gambled and ate up all his pay. He wouldn't ever amount to anything but a loser following the horses around the country. Jake remembered how surprised the owners were when Angelos was found with those bloody clothes. They said Angelos was quiet and great with the horses. Although he was a gambler, he worked hard and the track people all liked him.

But the DNA on the clothes matched the DNA of one of the women. And the mayor of Granelle wanted a quick end to the disappearances and the bloody crime scenes. With no alibi, the bloody clothes, and Angelos talking crazy about monsters, it was easy for the prosecution to get a quick conviction. But something always bothered Jake about the conviction and the evidence. The weird feeling that Jake felt at the Stanwick house, he felt four years before when he was searching for answers to those other cases. The problem was that everyone knew it.

Flipping through the file, Jake slowly looked at the crime scene photos. He remembered the dented car. But the grisly interior he hadn't seen. He paused at the picture of scratches on the hood of the car trying to decide what could have caused them. Jake flipped through the papers to the lab report. Jake frowned as he read the details about the DNA and the report about an unknown animal hair. As he continued turning pages, he was surprised to see in the file a copy of the lab report from Sharon Connor's case. The case he solved four years ago. Meg had highlighted parts of the report and made notations in the margins about a possible link between the two cases.

Jake closed the file. He picked up the statement that he had been given and signed his name on the bottom. He hated signing that paper and admitting that Jessie had assaulted Greg. He stood up taking the paper with him and walked to the booking area. Greg was still in his uniform, but was at the end of his shift and joking with someone Jake couldn't see. Jake ignored them and walked over to where Meg was sitting filing paperwork. He set the paper down and left without saying anything.

As Jake was walking out of the station, an older officer called out to him. Behind an old battered desk, Marty Driscole sat shuffling papers around. Having been wounded on the job, Marty had been relegated to maintaining old case files and sifting through forensic evidence in lieu of an early retirement. Marty had been sitting behind that desk since before Jake had been on the force.

"Hey, Jake, how's life?"

"Fine, fine. How have you been? Aren't you ready for retirement yet?"

"Can't keep an old cop down you know," Marty said laughing. Jake laughed with him.

"I've been thinking a lot about you. I've been looking for old case files that you worked on several years ago."

"Solved or unsolved?"

"Solved. It was those disappearances that happened about four summers ago. Douglas Angelos was convicted."

"Oh," Jake said losing interest.

"Riley took it a couple of weeks ago. Said there was a tie in to a new case. And Bennett came down looking for it this morning too."

"Well, I've got to get going. It was good seeing you again, Marty."

"Riley's got this crazy idea and she must be pumping it to Bennett. Something about weird animals stalking the night in Granelle." Marty laughed again. "She's really talking weird. Everyone's saying so."

"I really got to go. I'll see you later, okay."

"Sure, sure," Marty turned back to his papers.

Jake turned and left the building and found himself really concerned about Meg. She had been talking to Reggie about a strange theory and people were talking about her. As he crossed the parking lot, Jake saw Pete getting into his car and called out to him.

"Hey, Pete, wait up." Pete stopped and walked toward Jake. "What's going on with the Stanwick case?"

"Big case. You're missing out. But I hear the boss wants you back on the force."

"How is the investigation going? I heard Meg is on it."

"She's on it alright," Pete said with a tight laugh. "Strange ideas she has too."

"She's asking me some questions about an old case of mine and…"

"Oh, yeah. I know about it. She thinks the Rowley and Stanwick cases are connected to those disappearances a few years ago."

"I heard that Bennett thinks they might be connected too."

"Yeah. He talked to both of us about it. That's why he wants you back."

"You buy the theory that they are connected?"

"I'm following a few theories of my own. Riley's following hers."

"What's that mean? You're her partner, aren't you working together on the case?"

Pete looked uncomfortable. "Look Jake things are different now. We've had some recent vacancies on the force. Now, Crandall's moving downstate. Bennett's broken us up since were the only two detectives left."

"Pete, I'm not new around here. Why would Bennett break you up and have you both working the same cases? What's going on?"

"I don't know what to think. This is a bizarre case. We found a bashed up car in a garage, tons of blood, but no sign of forced entry. When Riley showed me the old file on your case, there were definite similarities. Angelos was convicted on circumstantial evidence and she said that you were never comfortable with the case against him."

"Even if there is a connection to the old case, I'm concerned that the evidence is getting lost in the searching for some connection. Why aren't you trying to get her to pursue other leads?"

Pete put up his hands defensively. "Whoa, is this Jake the detective or Jake the preacher. You want the case, Bennett would be glad to give you your badge back."

Jake sighed, "I can't do that."

"Hey, Buddy, I'm still your friend, regardless of your job. But unless you want to work with us, let us do our job."

"Pete, I just don't know what to do. I feel so drawn to the force, to the investigation. But I have an obligation to the church and to a calling that I feel that I have from the Lord."

"Maybe you should talk to someone about this that isn't biased."

"What do you mean?"

"Well, if you talk to Bennett, he will tell you to come back and join the force. If you talk to the old preacher, he will tell you to stay at the church. Who is the one person that you can lay all your concerns out to that will give you an unbiased opinion? Who do preachers talk to when they have a question or uncertainty?"

"I guess that would be God."

"You don't sound so sure."

Jake shook his head. "No, I'm sure. I think you just gave me the reason I'm struggling. Guess I need to pray about this."

"Hey, man, that's what friends are for. Even if I don't understand your answer. Got to go. It's been a long day."

Jake stood and watched as Pete drove off, knowing he needed to spend some time in prayer. The front door of the station swung opened and Meg and Greg Matthews jumped in a cruiser and left with the lights flashing. Reggie stood in the door watching them drive away. Jake walked back to the station.

"Another missing person?" Jake asked.

Reggie kept watching the car as is drove out of the long dusty drive and nodded. "Only a kid this time."

"Oh," Jake said and started walking toward his car.

"Peterson," Reggie called out. Jake stopped and looked back. "Might want to know that it's Sam Craig. I think his family goes to your church too."

"Yeah, they do. I'd better get over there," Jake hesitated. "Reg, what's the address."

"It's on Dunning Road. I think we may need to talk if we find out our first victim is one of your parishioners, too."

"I don't know how much help I can be. Remember I just started working there two months ago. I'm just getting to know the people."

"I'll be in touch," Reggie said going back inside.

CHAPTER 11

Karen led Jake into the kitchen were Meg and Greg were interviewing the Craigs. Jake knew as soon as he saw the Craigs who they were. Although he didn't know their daughter Karen, he recognized Stanley and Clara as the couple that always sat in the back, with their son between them, and left right after church was over. Clara was sobbing in a tissue and Stanley stood by her chair looking nervous and uncomfortable.

Meg didn't see Jake come in the room and she was continuing to question the Craigs. "When was the last time you spoke to your son, Mrs. Craig?"

"I already told you," she said into her tissue. "It was just before lunch."

"Knowing that he was a troubled child, why would you leave him here alone all day?"

"Officer, our son was not troubled. He got in trouble at school…," Stanley began and then noticed Jake standing in the doorway. "Oh thank God. Rev. Peterson, please tell these officers that our son was not a bad kid."

Meg whipped around and glared at Jake. "I'm sorry for interrupting. I was at the police station on another matter and the captain told me about Sam. I came to see if there was something I could do to help."

Stanley walked over to Jake and shook his hand. Clara cried louder and Meg said, "Perhaps this isn't a good time for your minister to be here, Mr. Craig. I'm investigating your son's disappearance."

Stanley looked nervously at Meg and then back at Jake. Jake put his hand on Stanley's shoulder. "I think that the Craigs just want some help finding him first. Then you can ask them all the questions you want. I can call the church and round up some people to help us search the woods for Sam. Is that alright with you, Stanley?"

"Yes," he said in relief. "I just want Sam home. If we were wrong to leave him home today, we'll make other arrangements. You can use the phone in my office," Stanley said leading Jake down the hall.

Out of earshot of the kitchen, Stanley whispered, "I didn't want to leave him home, Pastor Jake. But Clara...she felt we needed to teach him a lesson. He got in trouble at school yesterday. Please help us. I'm worried because he said there was an animal in the woods yesterday that scared him, and I just want him home before dark."

"It's going to be alright Stanley. Why don't we pray before I make that call? Is that okay?"

"Yes, please." The two men bowed their head in the hall and Jake prayed for Sam's safety. Meg started down the hall and stopped short when she saw Jake praying with Stanley. Not knowing what to do, she turned and went into the living room.

Jake finished his prayer and went into the office to call the church. When Mrs. Baxter answered the phone, Jake couldn't say a word.

"It's about time you finally checked in. It is highly irregular for you to be out so long. Why Pastor Walt wouldn't have even gone to that trailer park. He would have just let the police handle this," when she stopped for a breath Jake interrupted her.

"Sam Craig is missing."

"What? What did you say?" she said exasperated.

"Stanley and Clara Craig's son is missing. He must be only about 10 or 11 years old. You know them...they sit in the back pew. Can you call around and see if anyone is available to help search the woods in back of the Craigs' house? We would really like to have Sam home by dark."

"Well are the police there yet?"

"Yes, they are. But the department only has a handful of officers. The woods around the Craig's house are dense and the police can't possibly cover that much area. Besides, they spent a good part of yesterday searching for Kathy."

"Oh," she said quietly. "I'll see if Coach Morgan is at the high school. Maybe we can round up some of the teens to help."

"Thank you, Mrs. Baxter. And would you mind asking people in the church to pray for Sam's safe return home?"

"You didn't need to even ask me that. My second call would have been to the prayer chain. But I still need you to come by the church office before I go home. There are several things that I need you to look at."

"I'll try."

"No…don't try. Just come, Pastor Jake. Oh, and what is the title of the sermon? I need to finish the bulletin before I can go home."

"I'm not sure yet."

"Please give me something. My husband is used to having dinner at a certain time…."

"Okay, okay. Just call it Trusting."

"Trusting…trusting what?"

"Just trusting. I'll fill in the blank with the sermon." With that, Mrs. Baxter hung up the phone without saying good-bye.

Jake looked at the receiver in his hand. Someone cleared his throat and Jake turned and saw Greg at the door. "Sorry to bother you. Riley's hot and she just called Bennett. She's saying you're interfering in our investigation."

"Don't worry about it. The whole football team should be here soon to help find Sam. Mrs. Baxter is calling the coach. His parents are members of our church and most of the kids know who Karen is at least."

"Okay. I'll let Bennett know that when he gets here. You might want to get out of here before he gets here."

"Why would I do that? Bennett told me to come here and see if they needed any help."

"Oh, I don't think Riley knew that."

"I mentioned that the captain told me about Sam and he knew I was coming here. Anyway, let's go out and see if we can get this search started," Jake followed Greg back down the hall to the living room where Meg was questioning Stanley again. Jake heard them talking about the animal that Stanley mentioned to him in the hall and the urgency to get the search going. A car pulled into the driveway and Jake and Greg used it as an excuse to go outside.

Coach Morgan got out of the car along with several teens with school jackets. Two other cars pulled up behind the coach's car filled with more teens. Karen came out in a heavy coat and work boots. A couple of the boys who knew her went over and asked about her brother. Greg rounded up the boys and began to give them directions about beginning the search. Coach Morgan walked over to Jake and shook his hand.

When he knew that the kids couldn't hear him he said, "So, this is, what, the third missing person in Granelle? Are these all connected?"

"I don't know any more than you do Coach."

"Aw come on. You were on the force...."

"That's the operative word...were. I'm not anymore. So, I don't get insider information. All I know is that the Craigs are really worried about their son. Thanks for coming so quickly. Why don't we join the searchers?"

"Don't give me the bum's rush, Pastor Jake. Is there something going on in Granelle? People are getting scared again...just like before."

Jake put up his hands in mock surrender. "Honestly. I don't know anything."

Coach Morgan looked Jake over and then nodded. "Okay, you don't know anything official. But you used to be a cop...what does your instinct tell you?"

Jake shrugged. "I guess what's bugging me is that there are two people missing from our church. Maybe it is a coincidence. Maybe Sam ran away because he was in trouble at school. But I know that I'm going to keep on praying."

"I didn't even think of that. Do you want me to check on this school problem? Think it might help?"

"Not right now. Let's just get into the woods and start looking. I have a really bad feeling about all this, especially with Pastor Walt just having surgery."

"But that's why the board brought you on. You're here to fill in the gap."

"I just hope that I can. Pastor Walt has big shoes to fill."

Coach laughed at that and slapped Jake on the back. "Who better than you? God knew what He was doing when He brought you back to Granelle. You aren't Walt...but he's not you either. Okay now, where'd my team get to?"

Jake and Coach walked to the woods and followed the voices that were calling Sam's name. Neither man saw the dark creature that watched from the tree line. It growled low when it saw Jake and slipped into the woods going in the opposite direction of the searchers.

Meg stepped out of the house with Stanley and saw a shadow disappearing behind the detached garage. Meg walked toward the woods trying to see if it was Sam. A car pulled up and distracted Meg. As the captain got out, Meg looked back to the woods, but the moment was gone.

CHAPTER 12

Clara rolled over in the empty bed. She could care less that Stanley wasn't home, but knowing that Sam was out there somewhere kept her awake. Knowing that she was going to be interviewed by all three local television stations in the morning, she hadn't had her usual sleeping pills. There was no sense going on TV with one of her headaches that the pills gave her. But she kept thinking about the bottle of pain killers that Stanley had after his back went out in the spring.

Clara got out of bed and looked out the window. She could see the flashlights from the searchers glowing in the darkness. Clara walked out into the hall and looked in on Karen. Karen was asleep buried under the covers. Clara pulled her door closed before she headed to the stairs. She turned the light on in the downstairs bathroom and opened the medicine cabinet. She looked at several half filled bottles of pills until she found the one she was looking for. Taking the cap off the bottle, she dumped two pills into her hand and filled a cup with water. She swallowed the two pills and started to put back the bottle. Hesitating, Clara dumped two more pills in her hand and swallowed them.

Clara filled the glass with water and took the glass into the living room. Sinking into Stanley's lounge chair, she thought about the last conversation she had on the phone with Sam. She knew something was wrong, why hadn't she trusted her instincts. Clara closed her eyes waiting to feel the effects of the pills. She had to look the part of the concerned parent tomorrow on TV, especially after she was portrayed as a neglectful parent for leaving an eleven year old home alone all day.

Clara emptied the glass as she thought about the probing questions that the detective kept asking her. Then, to make matters worse, that new preacher shows up and talks to Stanley. She knew he was the ex-cop turned religious and she didn't trust what side he was on. Oh, how could they understand how embarrassing it was that her son hit the teacher and got expelled from school?

They couldn't understand that she had to work and had no one that Sam could stay with. If anything happens to Sam, she could find herself charged with neglect. Clara stumbled back to the kitchen to refill the glass. Maybe if she fell asleep, she could forget at least for tonight how her life was spiraling out of control.

Clara went to the sink and looked out the window at the lights from the searchers again, knowing they were out there in the middle of the night looking for her son. As she stared out into the darkness, some of the lights looked red. She closed her eyes thinking the pills were finally working. When she opened them, she realized she was still holding the glass and she set it in the sink. She started walking back to the living room when a knock at the kitchen door startled her.

With her heart pounding, Clara turned toward the door expecting to see the police. They would arrest her for sure. Something must have happened to Sam. But she recognized Trevor standing at the back door and felt confused. She opened the door.

"Clara, I was out with the searchers and saw the light. Is everything alright?" he asked.

Clara felt herself sway and Trevor reached out and steadied her. At his touch, Clara began to tremble.

In a soft voice full of tenderness, Trevor said, "Sam will be fine."

Clara sobbed, "It's not just Sam. My whole life is awful." Tears began streaming down her face. The affects of the day began to hit her as she began to talk. "I was supposed to marry someone else. He was handsome and had money. But I got pregnant and he dumped me. I even had an abortion, but he still didn't want me. I only married Stanley so everyone would think it didn't matter that Ray ran out on me. But it mattered, it really mattered."

Clara turned her tear stained face up to Trevor. He was so handsome. She leaned against him. He moved out of the doorway and closed the door behind him. Gently, he took Clara into his arms and she laid her head against his chest. He reached up and smoothed her hair. Clara began to calm under his touch. She looked back up at him and drew him closer to her. The kiss was passionate and deep. Clara felt her pulse quicken and a warm sensation spread through her. It was a feeling that she hadn't felt in a very long time.

Trevor broke the kiss. "Clara, I need to get back out and look for Sam."

"No," she said her voice husky. She tried to pull him back into her embrace.

"I really need to go, Clara."

"Please don't leave me. I need someone."

"My concern is for Sam."

"What about me?"

"Certainly, you can come with me, Clara."

Caught off guard, Clara gasped, "With you?"

"Yes, you can come into the woods with me."

Looking into his eyes, she felt herself drawn to him again. She took a deep breath, smelling the scent from the woods and something wild coming from Trevor. She clung to him, suddenly aware that she was only wearing a nightgown. He brushed her cheek with the back of his fingers and pulled out of her grasp. He turned and opened the door and stepped out onto the stoop. Clara brought her hands to her throat and felt tears press against her eyelids. Trevor turned and put his hand out.

"Come with me." Clara put her hand in his and he drew her to him. He reached in back of her and closed the door. Walking through the darkness, Clara held onto Trevor's hand. She suddenly felt frightened and held tighter to his hand.

"Don't you have a flashlight?" she whispered. Trevor didn't answer, but kept walking toward the woods. Clara tried to let go of his hand as they reached the woods, but he held tight. Clara stumbled forward and branches scratched her face. Trevor picked up his pace and she struggled to keep up with him. Deeper and deeper they went into the woods. Suddenly Trevor let go of her hand and stepped away. Clara stopped confused in the darkness.

"Trevor?" her voice trembled. "Where are you?"

There was no reply. Trevor stood a few feet away from her waiting and watching. There was a rustling of leaves behind Clara and she turned to the sound. "Trevor?" A low growl answered her. She saw the glowing red eyes looking up at her. She gasped and turned running blindly away. Trevor kept pace with her as the creature chased her toward the ravine. Tripping on her slippers, Clara fell, but quickly got back on her feet. The haze had long abandoned her and she screamed as she felt hot breath on the back of her legs.

The creature moved to her left causing Clara to veer the other way. Close to the edge of the ravine Clara fell again. Lying feeling too exhausted to continue, Clara began to cry. But when the creature sniffed at her a low moan erupted from her and she rolled away. Forcing herself to get back on her feet,

Clara ran off the edge of the ravine. As she fell, she smacked her head into the rock wall. Stunned by her head injury, she was unaware of the breaking of her back as her body crumpled at the bottom. Mercifully, Clara blacked out.

Trevor stood at the top of the ravine and turned on the flashlight. The light bathed over the crumpled body and he snapped it off. The creature began to scale down the cliff.

"No, she's not prey," Trevor said to the creature. It looked up at Trevor and growled. "Leave her be. She's not for you."

The creature came up to Trevor and sat down. It wined and pawed at Trevor.

"If you take the woman, we lose the boy. The boy is key to your survival. Come the other waits." Trevor turned away from the creature. The creature looked back down at Clara. He sniffed in the air and smelled the fresh blood. In its aggravation, it howled into the night. Trevor stopped and looked back at the creature.

"You will alert the humans. Hunt later. We've been away too long." Trevor turned back and continued to walk away. The creature paced at the top of the ravine. It no longer could see Trevor but knew he was still in the woods. The creature scaled down the ravine and stopped over Clara's lifeless body. It lapped at the blood that rolled down her cheek and whined softly. Finally, it turned away leaving Clara and raced back to the house.

The creature reached the house first and waited for Trevor to come out of the woods. Trevor walked up to the back door and took out a set of keys. He unlocked the door and entered the back hallway of the old house. Boxes lined the hallway leading into the main part of the house. Trevor hadn't bothered unpacking knowing their stay would be short in Granelle. He relocked the door and then threw a deadbolt. The basement door was to the right and the creature waited for Trevor to open that one as well.

Trevor opened the door and the creature bolted down the stairs. Its claws made scraping sounds on the cold cement floor. Trevor followed the creature down to the basement. These rooms were the ones that they had been living in and it smelled foul. Trevor looked at the other creature as it lay on the blankets on the floor. He approached her and knelt down. Gently he stroked her coarse fur. An old man came out of the small interior room. He was wearing old ripped jeans and a dirty plaid shirt. He swiped a dirty hand across his heavy jowls and shook his head at Trevor.

"She's not well," the old man said as he pulled an old bandana out of his back pocket. He used it to wipe his hands on as he knelt down next to Trevor. The old man gently ran a hand down her back until it came to a large wound on her hind quarter.

"Shamus, when the car hit her, I didn't think it hurt her this badly," Trevor said watching Shamus gently examine the wound.

"Aye, it is bad," Shamus said in his heavy brogue. His eyes were bloodshot and watery from sleepless nights.

Trevor glanced around and nodded toward an outer room. "Where did the other one go? In the back room?"

"Aye."

"Will she survive?"

"I think an infection has gotten her. But it's hard to tell. We really need a vet."

"You know that's out of the question. Will nourishment help?"

"Perhaps. If she can take it."

"What about him?"

"Be careful, he may be dangerous if something happens to her."

Trevor nodded. He continued to stroke the creature. Deep emotions shook him as he watched her shallow breathing. He had lived a long time with the creatures, caring for them. This would be difficult. He looked up and found the male watching him. The creature approached and lay down near her face. He reached a forefoot out and touched her face. At his touch, she opened her eyes and sighed. Trevor got up and went to the far side of the room. He opened a crate and pulled out some dried meat. He sat down in one of the chairs that he had brought down from the kitchen and took a bite of the meat. When he was finished he went up the stairs.

In the old dining room, Shamus had left Trevor's folded clothes. Trevor changed into a pair of jeans and a white button down shirt. He pulled his keys and wallet out of the dirty pair and threw the dirty clothes in a pile in the corner. He took the money out of the wallet and counted it. Satisfied, he tucked it back in and put the wallet in his back pocket. He took the black jacket that was hung over a chair and slipped it on. As he sat to put his shoes back on, the creature entered the room.

Trevor sat back in the chair as the creature approached him. The creature sat down in front of Trevor waiting. Trevor wet his lips hesitating. Finally he began, "She got hurt really bad with that car in the garage."

The creature became very still as if understanding. "I'm going to do everything in my power to see that she gets well. I'm going to get her some fresh meat. Stay here with her. If you need me, Shamus will call me. I will come back."

The creature went back to the other. Trevor put his shoes on and headed out the door. He knew that the creature would hunt for himself later. But it was up to him to keep her alive. If she died, Trevor feared he would die also.

* * *

As he lay asleep in his cell in the prison in Coxsackie, Douglas Angelos watched Clara die. He watched through the eyes of the creature as it looked down the ravine at the crumpled woman. When he heard Trevor's voice call to the creature, he jerked awake. The scene vanished, but he knew it was real. He regretted the day that he befriended Trevor at the track. For the thousandth time, he berated himself for not trusting his instincts. The horses were terrified of Trevor and that should have been the first warning that Angelos heeded.

Now they were back, hunting again. The demons that he let in all those years before still tormented him causing him to see in his dreams the terrors that the creature caused. But the new knowledge of the darkness that was unfolding terrified him more than anything he had experienced before. Angelos tried to get people to listen, but no one would. They thought he was crazy. He had even tried to get Peterson to listen to him, but he never came.

Angelos reached under his pillow to feel the small book the Chaplin gave him three days ago. He had tried to read it, but he couldn't focus on the words. But he was too old and tired to take anymore of the nightmares. He pulled the book out and laid it on his chest. The tormenting voices filled his mind and he felt worthless. Taking a deep breath, he sobbed. He tried to remember what the chaplain had said to him.

Finally in desperation, Angelos started screaming. The guard came running down the hall. After a few frantic moments, Angelos was restrained and he was given a shot. Screams continued to fill his head, but he stopped struggling as the drugs took effect. Once he was sleeping he was taken to the infirmary.

* * *

Sam jerked awake and sat listening. Something woke him and he was unsure what it was. He crawled toward the cave opening and looked out into the night. The searchers had headed home for the night and it was dark. Feeling uneasy, Sam regretted his decision to run away from home. He kept thinking about Trevor's dogs with the red eyes and felt scared. He would go home at first light and lie about running away. After all, kids got lost in the woods all the time. Getting back into his father's sleeping bag, Sam glanced at his watch it was just past midnight. It would be another long night.

CHAPTER 13

Stanley woke up stiff from sleeping on the couch. When he finally got home around 1:00 in the morning, he didn't want to wake up Clara. He looked at the clock on the wall and realized he needed to get moving. The first searchers would begin around 7 am and he wanted to be there.

As Stanley started up the stairs, he heard Karen's alarm clock going off. He hurried to beat her into the bathroom. As he turned on the shower, Karen knocked on the door. He yelled that he was in the shower and Karen went back to her room. The warm water helped revive him and he lingered letting the water pour down his back. Finally he shut off the water, wrapped a towel around his waist, and went to the bedroom. Quietly he opened the door so that he wouldn't wake up Clara. He was surprised to find the bed empty and quickly got dressed. He ran a comb through his thinning hair and hoped Clara had started coffee.

Stanley went downstairs to the kitchen. Glancing around, he called out, "Clara? Where are you?"

He stood listening for a moment and then went to his den. "Clara? Are you alright?" When he didn't find her he began to frantically search the downstairs rooms calling her name louder.

"Dad?" Karen stood on the bottom step looking scared.

"Have you seen your mother?"

"No."

"I can't find her. I'm going to look outside."

Stanley went out the front door and looked around the yard. He ran to the driveway and saw her car was still parked next to his in front of the garage. He put his hand on the hood and found it cold.

"Clara!" he called out. Running to the backyard, he stopped short as he saw Sam step out of the woods. Sam stopped when he saw his father staring at him. He pulled the Walkman off his head.

"Dad, are you alright?" Sam asked. At the sound of his son's voice, Stanley ran to him and grabbed him in a hug. He began crying in relief and exhaustion.

"Dad?"

Stanley pulled back and looked down at his son. "It's really you? You came back?"

"I got lost yesterday. I'm sorry."

"Where were you?"

"I don't know. I was lost."

Stanley looked at him doubtful. "We've got some talking to do, I think. But I'm glad you're all right. You must be starved. Let's find you some breakfast."

Stanley put his arm around Sam's shoulder and walked toward the back door. When he opened the door, all the joy he felt about finding Sam was lost as he realized that Clara was gone. Karen looked up and gasped as she saw Sam walk in behind Stanley.

"Sam! Dad, you found Sam! Is Mom out there too?"

"Mom? What are you talking about?" Sam asked.

Stanley turned toward his son. "She must have gone out looking for you. She's not here."

Sam turned and ran out into the yard. "Mom!" he shouted. "I'm home. Come back!" Stanley and Karen joined Sam in the yard and began calling for Clara too. After a few minutes they stopped and looked at each other.

Stanley shook his head. "It's no use. If she were near enough to hear us, she'd be back already. I should go in and call the police and let them know that Sam is home."

Karen and Sam followed Stanley back into the house. Sam sat at the kitchen table and Karen went to make herself some breakfast. They could hear their father on the phone in the other room.

"Why'd you do it?" Karen asked softly.

Sam shrugged. "I was bored, so I took a walk and got lost."

Karen looked up at him. "Don't give me that line. I know you know these woods like the back of your hand. You had to know it would hurt Mom and Dad."

"I got lost." Karen and Sam stared at each other for a few long moments.

"Yeah, whatever," Karen said as she got up and threw out her breakfast.

Stanley walked into the kitchen and began looking in the refrigerator for eggs. There wasn't much in the refrigerator, but some old leftovers. He shook his head and pulled the almost empty milk carton out of the refrigerator.

"I guess cereal's out of the question. Any ideas?" he looked at his kids.

Karen shook her head. "I don't have time. I'm getting ready for school."

She started walking out and Stanley stopped her. "Maybe you should stay home today."

"No," she said shaking her head. "Mom will be back and I'm not missing school. It's bad enough that everyone in town thinks my brother is a delinquent. I'm not getting put in his category."

"Karen, that's uncalled for."

"Let her go Dad, she's right. I don't know how things got so bad this year. But I was thinking last night that somehow, it's got to get better. Ted's a jerk and no one sees it but me. But in trying to make everyone see what he's really like is making it look like I'm the jerk."

"You're not a total jerk," Karen said poking him in the shoulder, "just a partial."

Stanley didn't say anything as Karen left and went upstairs to get ready for school. Sam poked at a hole in the tablecloth feeling embarrassed that his Dad just stood there staring at him.

When Sam heard the shower start, he cleared his throat, "Pop-tarts. I'll just eat Pop-tarts. They don't need milk." He got up and opened a cupboard and found one left in the box. He put it in the toaster and threw the box and wrapper away. When he finally turned around, his father had left and gone to his study. Sam let his breath out. Man, he was lucky his mother wasn't home.

Sam sat eating his Pop-tart thinking about his night and the strange dreams. He wondered how a dream could seem so real. He looked down at his half eaten Pop-tart and his stomach rolled. Sam picked it up and threw it away.

Sam walked into the living room and sat on the couch. He flicked on the TV with the remote unaware of the cluttered room. He found the channel with the same newscaster that he watched the day before. Another beautiful day. Sam figured he'd be out finishing the lawn soon.

"Are you going to just sit on the blanket or put it away?" Karen asked from the bottom step. Standing with her hands on her hips and an annoyed look on her face, she looked just like a younger version of their mother.

"What?" Sam asked looking down at the couch.

"Men," Karen said rolling her eyes. She marched to the couch and yanked the blanket out from under Sam. She rolled it up and took the pillow and stuffed them into the closet. Then she disappeared down the hall to find Stanley. Sam found himself watching some old sitcom that made everyone look dorky. When the doorbell rang, Sam started to get up and Stanley practically ran down the hall waving him back into his seat.

Sam fell back onto the couch and listened as his father answered the door. Stanley walked into the room followed by Jake.

Stanley said, "Sam, this is Pastor Jake. Do you remember him from church?" Sam shrugged. "He wants to talk to you for a few minutes," Sam looked up at Jake and switched off the TV.

"Hi, Sam," Jake reached his hand out and Sam clumsily shook his hand. Jake sat on the opposite end of the couch. "We were all concerned about you yesterday. What happened?"

Sam sat up straighter on the couch and glanced around for Karen. He looked back at Jake and shrugged. "I don't know. I just got lost out there."

"You go in the woods often?"

"Yeah."

"How'd you get lost?"

Sam shrugged again and looked down at the couch. "I was kind of mad and wasn't paying attention to where I was going and…I don't know." Sam began picking at a string on the couch. Jake waited for him to go on.

"Sam, Pastor Jake is here trying to help us," Stanley urged him taking a step closer to the couch. Sam looked at his father feeling nervous.

Sam looked back at the string and began pulling it again. "I…just started walking and looking around at stuff. I got lost."

"How did you find your way back?" Jake asked.

"I started walking around this morning and just recognized something and realized where I was."

"There were searchers out for hours last night and late into the night. Didn't you hear anyone calling for you?"

The doorbell rang and Stanley went to answer it. Sam waited not knowing if he should wait for his father.

"Sam?" Jake prodded. Sam looked up as Karen came downstairs. She stopped, watching her father at the door.

"Pastor Jake, there is an officer here that wants to talk to me. Can you stay?"

"Of course," Jake said.

"Kids go upstairs for now." Sam was relieved to get away from the probing questions and followed his sister up the stairs to her room.

Greg Matthews nodded at Jake and waited until Stanley sat down in the recliner. Greg cleared his throat and glanced at Jake, "Mr. Craig, I've got some bad news. Some of the searchers had already started looking for your son this morning. They found a woman at the bottom of the ravine. It looks like your wife."

"Is she?" Stanley said hesitating.

"Yes, looks like her neck is broken. We need you to come down to the morgue and identify the body."

Stanley stared at Jake for a moment as if unable to comprehend what he just heard. He took off his glasses and put his face in his hands. Jake went over to Stanley and put his hand on his shoulder. "Stanley, they don't know for sure. Is Clara here?"

"No, I was looking for her when Sam walked out of the woods and then I forgot."

"Excuse me," Greg interrupted. "Is Sam back?"

"Yes, he just went upstairs with his sister."

"Oh, I didn't even realize it because of finding…well…," Greg stammered. "I guess I should radio in and let the searchers know the boy has come home. We're going to need to talk to him, especially with his mother.…"

Stanley looked up and put his glasses back on. "I don't understand."

Jake stopped him. "It's alright Stanley. Right now, let's find out if this is Clara. We'll take this one thing at a time. Is that okay with you officer?"

Greg nodded. "Is there someone you can call to stay with the children?"

Stanley shook his head. "No. All our family lives out of town. There is no one to call."

"I can stay with the children," Jake said. "If that's okay with you Stanley. I won't say anything about Clara until you come back and we are sure."

Stanley stood to leave and felt dizzy. He sat back down. "Pastor Jake, I have a sister in Poughkeepsie. Maybe Karen can find the number. I…I…," Stanley broke down and cried.

It was a long hard day for the Craigs and Jake stayed with them. When Reggie came and asked questions, Jake sat with the kids on the couch listening while Stanley told Reggie about their marital problems. He sat with Sam when Meg showed up grilling him about being lost. It was Jake who called the funeral home and began the early preparations. He knew that he had a sermon to still prepare for, but the family didn't know what to do. When the police and news crews finally left, Jake even ordered pizza for dinner that hardly anyone ate.

Finally as dusk began to settle, Stanley's sister, Sheryl, and her husband, Kyle, arrived from Poughkeepsie. Karen, who spent most of the day crying, threw her arms around her aunt and sobbed. Sam sat next to Jake on the couch and didn't move. As Sheryl and Kyle carried their suitcases to the spare room upstairs, Jake finally felt it was time to leave. Jake stood at the door saying good-bye to Stanley and Sam finally started to cry. As he drove the back road to his little house, Jake prayed for the family and the hard days ahead.

CHAPTER 14

After a long tiring night, Jake stood on the platform near the pulpit and looked at the congregation. He saw George Stanwick flanked by his parents in the row he normally sat with Kathy. Sitting between his parents, Jake could picture George as a small boy. His parents sat stoically, apparently not approving of Jake's guitar playing. Normally, Millie played the piano while the congregation sang worship songs. But Millie was staying in Albany with her daughter while Pastor Walt recovered from his open heart surgery.

Jake began to play a new song and Mrs. Baxter tried to find the words on the transparency for the overhead. She had made a list of songs that she thought went along with his sermon title, "Just Trusting," and handed it to Jake this morning. Jake had decided that they should allow the Holy Spirit to guide them. Now, she struggled with keeping up with the changes and trying to find the songs in her box of transparencies. Although Jake tried to talk to Walt about getting a computer program that would display the words using a projector, Walt felt that the church wasn't ready for fancy technology.

Jake sang the familiar song and silently prayed for the small group that was gathered. So many families were missing this morning, including the Craigs. Stanley was home with his children mourning the loss of his wife. Jake tried placing the names of the absent members, but did notice a few newer faces. Coach Morgan sat with a group of teens that had helped search for Sam a few days ago. Finally, Jake ended the song and one of the elders came up on the platform as Jake set his guitar to the side.

As Jake took a seat on the front pew, he smiled his thanks to Mrs. Baxter, but she was busy trying to get the transparencies back in the box.

"As you all know by now, Pastor Walt is in the hospital," Elder Dave Jacobs began.

Dave had been a member of Granelle Gospel since he was a boy. Now in his mid-fifties, Dave had attended the church longer than any other member.

Dave was one of the elders that whole-heartedly supported the decision to hire Jake. A few had objected to Jake taking the position since he was single, but Dave was single and argued that shouldn't be a consideration. Besides Jake wasn't a stranger to Granelle and Dave had known Jake when he was a detective.

Dave ran his hand through his thinning grey hair, a gesture that everyone knew. He was short and stocky and looked uncomfortable in his suit and tie. Jake told him it wasn't necessary, but Dave insisted since he was going to give the announcements this morning. Usually Jake did the announcement, but Dave felt that it was too much for Jake to do the entire service. Dave glanced at Jake for support and Jake smiled.

Dave cleared his throat and continued. "But that doesn't mean we won't have our regular services. That's why we hired Pastor Jake to fill in when we have a need. I see many vacant seats today and we need to let everyone know that the church will continue to run as usual. And of course, Mrs. Baxter will be helping Pastor Jake and the elders too. Okay now, we have a few regular announcements. We have our ladies auxiliary holding its fall potluck supper on November 2. We have a signup sheet in the bulletin. Sign up early so that the ladies have time to make their plans. Our regular Wednesday night prayer meeting is on. We have a lot of prayer needs in the church so we need all the prayer warriors to come out and pray."

As Dave continued to go through the list of upcoming events, Jake sat fidgeting. This was only his second sermon since he came back to Granelle. He felt ill prepared for today and it didn't help him that Mrs. Baxter put the Just in front of Trusting as a sermon title. That little word made a big difference in the meaning of what Jake should say. He thought about Proverbs 3:5-6 that he was going to use as his basis for the sermon and felt it wasn't right now.

Jake bowed his head as Dave led the congregation in prayer and then opened his Bible as the ushers began collecting the offering. Dave looked at Jake as the ushers reached the back of the church and noticed he was reading the Word. Not wanting to make Jake look bad, Dave began to sing. In his deep baritone, Dave sang out the old hymn. It surprised everyone including Jake. As Jake recognized the song, he stood and sang with Dave. Mrs. Baxter fumbled with the overhead and everyone stood with Jake and sang.

"Simply trusting every day, trusting through a stormy way, Even when my faith is small, Trusting Jesus, that is all. Trusting as the moments fly, Trusting as the days go by; Trusting Him whate'er befall, Trusting Jesus, that is all (hymnlyrics.org)."

When the song was over, Dave went to his seat and everyone settled waiting for Jake as he stood behind the pulpit. He bowed his head and began to pray as for God's presence to be in their midst. A few murmurs of agreement reached Jake and he felt encouraged.

"I want to begin by reading Psalm 112. 'Blessed is the man who fears the LORD, who finds great delight in his commands. His children will be mighty in the land; the generation of the upright will be blessed. Wealth and riches are in his house, and his righteousness endures forever. Even in darkness light dawns for the upright, for the gracious and compassionate and righteous man. Good will come to him who is generous and lends freely, who conducts his affairs with justice. Surely he will never be shaken; a righteous man will be remembered forever. He will have no fear of bad news; his heart is steadfast, trusting in the LORD. His heart is secure, he will have no fear; in the end he will look in triumph on his foes. He has scattered abroad his gifts to the poor, his righteousness endures forever; his horn will be lifted high in honor. The wicked man will see and be vexed, he will gnash his teeth and waste away; the longings of the wicked will come to nothing.'"(NIV)

"Our little church has certainly had its share of bad news this past week. It started with Pastor Walt's heart attack. If that had been the only trial we faced this week, it would have been a lot. But no." Jake looked down at George and stepped away from the pulpit. He walked off the platform. "Our friend Kathy is missing, too. George and Kathy are a big part of our little church. I know that I appreciate all that George does behind the scenes here." A few of the men murmured agreements. George looked down at his hands and his mother put her arm around him.

"Kathy has been a wonderful part of our children's program. Her kindness and gentle way has reached the hearts of many of our children. But more than they do around the church is their love of the Lord and their friendship. Then to add to our bad news, Clara Craig passed away in an accident yesterday." A few gasps went up from the congregation. Jake looked around to see a few surprised looks. "I'm sorry. I thought that everyone knew about Clara."

Jake looked down at the Bible that was in his hands and then went on. "How easy it would be for us to look at these two families and ask God 'why'. To stop trusting that God will work everything out for good. I sat at home last night and wondered what I could say to you this morning. What I had been planning on saying didn't seem to fit after I came home from the Craigs. It feels like, to me, that a darkness has settled on our little town of Granelle. We have another missing woman and the police force is scrambling to try to make sense of this for everyone. Fear has seized us. People are locking themselves in at dusk. People are asking me what is happening. So, what can I say to you? To you who are afraid? To the Craigs? To George?" Jake hesitated and shook his head. "I can say nothing."

Jake walked back to the pulpit. The room was silent. He set his Bible down and looked up at the people. He looked at the Stanwicks and felt such compassion.

"I have nothing that I can say to any one of you. But God does. He tells us to trust Him. We just read Psalm 112 where it said that 'Even in darkness, light dawns for the upright and he will have no fear of bad news; his heart is steadfast, trusting in the LORD. His heart is secure, he will have no fear; in the end he will look in triumph on his foes.' Our light in this darkness our town is facing is the Lord Jesus Christ. We have nothing to fear because we have the Lord on our side. We have to simply trust in Him. Does that just seem like empty words to you? The word trust means to have confident expectation of something, hope, or a person on which one relies. I have hope that good will come out of this. I have hope that God will be glorified in the end."

"Amen," George said. Jake noticed others nodded in affirmation. "There are other verses I could give you about trusting or hope. I want to look at the life of Job. Certainly, it looked like Job had little hope with all he went through from the loss of his wealth to the death of his children." Jake turned in his Bible to the book of Job. He went on to talk about all the trials that Job endured.

"As I conclude today, I think that we need to have a time of prayer. We need to agree in prayer for the safety of this town, for the safety of Kathy, for Pastor Walt's healing and that the darkness will be lifted and the wicked person who is responsible will be found and brought to justice. I want everyone to just come forward so we can gather together and pray."

Jake walked off the platform again and waited while everyone gathered up in the front. A few of the older people sat in the first pews. Jake led in prayer and others prayed too. An hour quickly passed and they continued to pray for the town. A few people quietly left, but the core of the church remained into the early afternoon.

CHAPTER 15

The next few days were a blur to Sam. Mostly he sat in his house while relatives he didn't even know walked around him in dark clothes. He knew that they all heard about his trouble in school. A few even glared at him like it was his fault his mother was dead. Karen spent most of the time crying and his dad was walking around like a ghost. His aunt kept trying to make him eat something. But Sam couldn't eat. Even if the relatives hadn't accused him, he felt guilty anyway. He didn't need their silent accusations.

The police had come and asked what seemed to Sam like a thousand questions. He stuck to his story of being lost. He didn't even go back to the woods to get his stuff and no one noticed anything was missing. His mother would have, but no one else. Pastor Jake had been over every day to pray and talk with his father. A few times, he tried talking to Sam, but he sat silent and just stared. How could he talk to a man of God knowing his mother wouldn't have gone out that night to look for him if he hadn't run away?

Sam sat in the living room staring at a worn spot on the rug. He was wearing a new suit that his aunt had bought for him. The pants were too long and the shirt was too tight, but Sam didn't complain. Things were going to change soon, since his father already said they were moving to Poughkeepsie. So he was not only losing his mother, but everything he had known his whole life, his friends, his school, his room…everything.

"Sam, it's time to leave," his aunt said. Sam watched her pull on black gloves and wondered why she was wearing all black anyway. Karen came downstairs with a black dress on and no makeup. Sam stood up and walked to the door. His aunt clucked her tongue. "Just look at how handsome you are," she said with a sad smile. "The spitten image of your father at your age."

Sam looked at Karen who rolled her eyes behind her aunt's back. A car beeped its horn and she ushered the children to the door. A long black car sat in front of the house and Stanley was talking to the driver. The driver opened the door and the family got in.

It was a quiet ride to the church with everyone lost in thought. The parking lot at Granelle Gospel Church was packed. Sam didn't even think that his family knew that many people. He climbed out of the car and his father took his hand, something he hadn't done in years. Sam looked up at his father surprised and saw he was in tears.

One of the ushers, who Sam remembered as his mother's cousin, led them into the church. The cousin took his aunt's arm and Karen followed them to the front, but Sam just stopped and looked. Everyone was looking at them and he felt embarrassed. Certainly everyone in the room blamed him for his mother's death. He saw the woman cop who had been so mean to him the morning his mother was found. He saw Johnny and Melinda sitting together with their parents staring at him. He recognized many people from church and people who worked with his parents.

Stanley leaned down and whispered to Sam, "It's alright, son. We need to sit in the front."

"Dad," Sam whispered back. "Please don't make me. Everyone is staring at me."

"I'm here with you."

Sam began to cry. "Please just let me sit in the back like we do for church."

Stanley stepped back into the foyer and knelt down in front of Sam. Sam threw his arms around his father neck and sobbed. Stanley rubbed Sam's back and whispered reassurances to him. Finally, Sam began to calm down and let go of his father. Stanley pulled out a handkerchief and handed it to Sam. Sam dried his eyes and looked up to see Jake standing near them.

"Are you both ready?" Jake asked.

"We're having a bit of a problem," Stanley said. "Sam doesn't want to sit in the front with the family."

"Tell you what, Stanley. Why don't you go join Karen? I'll talk to Sam. Okay?"

"Alright," Stanley said as he stood. He walked into the sanctuary. Sam looked up at Jake who smiled at him.

"Come on," Jake said. "I have a secret entrance to the church. That way, you don't have to walk in front of everyone."

"I just want to stay here."

"Well, that won't look right to everyone in the church. You know, letting your dad and Karen sit alone. Come on, it's going to be okay."

Jake walked to the door and Sam followed. When they were outside, Sam saw the hearse pulled up and began to cry again. Jake put his arm around him and guided him around to the side of the church. He went through the side door that went to the offices. Mrs. Baxter was sitting at her desk and looked up surprised. She nodded at Jake and went back to her work. When Sam saw Mrs. Baxter, he stopped crying and wiped his eyes on his father's handkerchief again.

"See this is where we work. You know Mrs. Baxter from church. This big office here is Pastor Walt's office. Mine is down that hallway. Plus we have a big conference room where we have some small meetings from time to time. Now, this hallway is like a secret passageway. It leads right to the platform in the front of the church. Come on, I'll show you."

Sam followed Jake down the hall. There were two doors at the end of the hall. Sam stopped as Jake reached out for the handle.

"Pastor Jake," Sam said in a small voice. "I'm afraid to go out there and face everyone."

"Now, why would you be afraid? Most of those people are your friends and family."

Tears welled up in his eyes again. "It's like everyone knows about me."

"And what would they know about you, Sam?"

"I...never mind. Can't I just stay here with Mrs. Baxter?"

"What's really bothering you?"

"Nothing."

"Sam, you might be able to hide what's going on inside of you from everyone, your dad and sister, your friends, but you can't hide from God. No matter what you did, God already knows."

Jake waited for Sam to say something. Sam fidgeted and balled up the handkerchief. "I was bad in school."

"That's not what this is about though. Somehow you feel responsible for what happened to your mother. Don't you?" Sam nodded. "What really happened that day, Sam?"

"I didn't do anything to my mother."

"I know you didn't. But you still feel like it's your fault."

"Yeah."

"That's because the day before, you ran away. Right?"

"How did you know?" Sam said looking surprised. "I didn't tell anybody. Not even my best friend."

"I used to be a cop. Did you know that?"

Sam's eyes got big and he looked surprised as he shook his head. "How can you be our minister then?"

"Well, when I was a cop, a friend of mine told me about Jesus. He told me that God loved me so much that He sent His Son to die for me. I asked Jesus to forgive me and then felt like God wanted me to tell other people that He loves them too."

"So you stopped being a policeman?"

"Yes. I went to Bible School and learned even more about God. The one thing I learned is that you can't hide the things that you do that are bad from God. He knows everything. But the important thing to remember is that no matter how bad you are, God loves you so much that He wants to forgive all the bad things you've done."

"He won't forgive me, though," Sam said glumly.

"There is nothing so bad that God can't forgive you. Jesus made the way when He died on the cross for you. God looks at all sin the same. Sin is sin. And Jesus paid the price for it all."

"Do you really believe that?"

"With all my heart. All you have to do is pray and ask God to forgive you. Do you want to do that?"

Sam thought for a moment and then shook his head. "I need to think about this for a while."

"Okay. But if you have any questions, you can ask me. Or ask your Dad."

"My dad knows about Jesus?"

"Yes, he does. I've been praying with him a lot this week."

"Oh," Sam said. "I wish I knew that before."

"Well, it's never too late. Now, if you go through that door, it will take you out by the organ and the front row where your dad is. I'll go through this one which goes to the platform. Okay?"

Sam nodded and opened the door. Jake waited a moment and breathed a quick prayer before going out in front of the congregation.

CHAPTER 16

A few hours later, Jake was standing in the cemetery. The service took longer than he planned, but he knew Stanley wanted him to talk about salvation. As the family and close friends gathered for the final moments, Jake saw a stranger standing near the line of cars. It surprised him and he faltered in his reading of the scriptures. Meg, who had come to the cemetery noticed and glanced over at Jake. She looked around the crowd and didn't see anything unusual. Jake noticed her looking around and wanted to point him out to her, but knew it would be inappropriate. He just continued with his reading and closed in prayer. When he looked up again, the man was gone.

Sam stood staring at the flowers. Karen was crying next to him and he refused to cry again in front of anyone. He knew that in the small group, Johnny and his parents were standing. He hoped that they were going back to his house with the other people so he could talk to Johnny about everything that had happened.

Sam watched as his father walked up to the casket and put a flower on it. Karen picked up a flower and did the same. There were a few moments of awkward silence as everyone waited for Sam to do the same. Karen nudged him and he finally went up too. Karen took his hand and began to walk him toward the cars. Sam tried to look around to see Johnny and watched as his parents lead him in the opposite direction. Sam felt disappointment wash over him and hung his head as he walked.

Jake tried to take in everything that was going on as he shook hands with the lingering mourners. He watched the Craigs get into the rented car and drive away. When the last of the mourners got in the cars, Jake walked to his truck. Meg was leaning up against the front of it.

"So, what was that stumble at the end about?" Meg asked as Jake walked up to her.

"There was a stranger standing by the cars. He wasn't at the funeral and I didn't recognize him. Did you see him?"

Instantly, Meg began looking around as the people were pulling out of the cemetery. "Where was he?"

"Long gone, Meg."

"Why didn't you tell me sooner so I could have checked him out?"

"And do what? Say…hey officer, there's a strange man by the cars. Ruin the final moments of this awful day for the family? The coroner ruled the death was accidental, from what the family told me."

"That doesn't mean anything when we still have two missing women in Granelle."

"Why are you here anyway?"

Meg pushed herself away from the truck. "I don't answer to you."

"Wait a minute," Jake said following her. "Do you think there is a connection between the Craigs and the disappearance?"

"Oh, now you're interested in the cases?" she asked sarcastically as she walked over to her car.

"No, I'm interested in the Craigs. They've just had a major loss in their lives. Everyone in that family is beating themselves up. Plus, they are members of my church."

"Well, just go back to your church. I don't have any answers for you."

Jake grabbed her arm and made her stop. "What's going on?"

Meg stared at Jake for a minute and then pulled her arm away. "Okay. The lab report on the Stanwick case came back conclusively that there were animal hairs caught on the molding of the car. Animal hairs, just like the ones found at the scene in the case that Angelos was convicted of."

"That's what you want to talk to me about?"

"Do you remember the night at the Stanwick house, someone told me that you said that there was something in the woods. Some animal?" When Jake didn't respond she went on. "What did you see? Could it have gotten Kathy Stanwick?"

"What do you mean, gotten her?"

"There's no body, remember?"

"Where are you going with this, Meg? Some animal opened the car door and ate Kathy Stanwick? Is that what you believe? Did the lab reports find animal saliva at the scene?"

"That's the problem. No saliva was found. Only a few hairs."

"So what do you want from me? Is this what Reggie wants me to look at?"

"What kind of animal did you see?

"It was nothing. A dog or something. Nothing that would have swallowed a human being."

"The hairs, though. Jake, they are a match to the hairs found in your old case records."

"Animal hairs. Animal hairs found at a crime scene in upstate New York in the Adirondack Mountains. How unusual is that? Could an animal have brushed up against her car at some time prior to her disappearance. Probably. Is it related to her disappearance? Probably not. A wild animal can't pick up humans, swallow them whole or make them disappear."

They stared at each other for a minute. "I should have expected that you wouldn't help me. You don't even want to see that there are similarities between this case and Angelos."

"It's not that I don't want to help you. But I don't know anything about this case. I'm not a cop anymore. I'm a minister with a church that I'm struggling to hold together right now."

"Would it help you to know that there were animal hairs on Mrs. Craig's clothing, too? And, that Mr. Craig told me about a wild animal around their house at the time of her untimely death?"

"Where are you going with this? What do animal hairs have to do with this?"

"I'm not sure. I'm just following a hunch right now. I found some information on the Internet about…never mind," she said turning away.

"Meg, are you trying to work a theory that this person has an animal? Like owns a wild animal?"

"Forget it, Jake," she threw over her shoulder. "I'll figure it out on my own."

Jake watched as she got in her car and drove away. He looked at his watch and knew he needed to stop at the reception at the Craigs and still get to the church before Mrs. Baxter left.

CHAPTER 17

Early the next morning, Jake had stopped at the Stanwicks before going to the church. He hadn't seen George since church on Sunday and had wanted to make sure that he was doing alright. The searchers had stopped combing the woods behind his house days ago and that bothered Jake. It was a week since Kathy disappeared and there was no information about her on the news.

Mrs. Stanwick answered the door and was cool toward Jake. She told him that George didn't need to be disturbed and that he should have called instead of stopping by. But George heard them and came out of a back room.

"Pastor Jake, I'm so glad you came by," George said as he reached out to shake Jake's hand.

"Are you sure this is a good time?" Jake asked, glancing at George's mother. George looked at his mother too and saw the disapproval on her face. George motioned to Jake to step outside and they went outside together. The early morning air was cold. George rubbed his hands on his arms.

"Sure is cold this morning. Makes me really worry about Kathy being out there somewhere," George said looking around at the woods around his house. "Kathy loves it up here. You probably don't know that it was her decision to move out here. She found the house...." George stopped his eyes filling with tears. Jake put his hand on George's shoulder.

"How's it going, George?" Jake asked.

"It's been really difficult. My mother thinks I should leave and go back with them to Saratoga. Since I won't leave the house, she's insisting on staying. She thinks she needs to protect me," he laughed a little sadly. "Guess she still thinks I'm her little boy or something. Not Kathy's husband."

"She's just concerned for you."

"I know that. But Kathy's my wife and I won't leave her. Plus Granelle is my town now, not Saratoga. And the church is my family."

"We all prayed for Kathy and you last night. I wanted so much to be here for you these past few days, but I had the funeral...."

"Pastor Jake, you don't need to explain. I know there are so many other things going on right now. I wanted to be at that prayer meeting last night. But my mother was afraid to stay home alone. The news has been awful and it scares her."

"She would have been welcome."

"I know that. But she doesn't approve of our church. She thought Sunday morning was wrong with the guitar and our prayers."

"I'm sorry you're going through all this."

George nodded. "It has been hard. I've been spending a lot of time in prayer and I keep going back and reading Psalm 112. I'm trusting that God will bring Kathy back to me."

"How's the investigation going?"

"That's the weird thing. I don't really know. That detective...Riley, she's here a lot asking me questions. I think at first, she thought I had something to do with this. But now, she's asking me questions about dogs and if I'm involved in any satanic cults."

"That is strange."

"I told her that we were church going people and not involved in anything like that."

"Hmm," Jake said thinking. "Well, just so you know, it's not unusual for the police to suspect a close family member in a disappearance. They do need to rule you out as a suspect."

"Yes, I guess so. Even so, I don't think they are going in the right direction with this. A few of the news stations want me to be interviewed with the Rowley family. They say it may help someone remember something. I don't feel right about it. Kathy disappeared from our garage. How could anyone have seen anything from that? The only reason I'm considering it is because maybe it will get the police to keep on looking for her."

"The news stations have their own agenda. Sometimes it can help an investigation, other times it's just to exploit a family for news ratings. Before you decide to do any interviews, talk to Captain Bennett. He's a fair man and if he thinks there is a good reason to do it, he will tell you."

The front door opened and both men looked to see Mrs. Stanwick standing with hands on her hips. "George, it's too cold to be standing out here and your coffee is getting cold."

"I should get going anyway," Jake said. He shook George's hand. "I'll be in touch."

"Call first," Mrs. Stanwick said from the door.

"I'll walk you to your car," George said walking toward the driveway.

"George!" his mother called as the two men walked away.

Once out of earshot, George said, "You are always welcome here. I'm putting an end to this today. I didn't realize how much I had let her take over until you came by."

"Call me if you need anything," Jake said. George stood by the new garage door and watched as Jake got in and drove away. Jake looked up the embankment where he had seen the creature disappear a week ago. With the early morning sun shining through the trees, the entire hill was washed in golden sunlight. Jake waved to George as he backed out onto the dirt road. He laughed when he saw Mrs. Stanwick walking around the corner of the house with George's coat.

As Jake's car headed down the road, Meg watched from her car near the bend in the opposite direction. She had come to discuss the case with George again, but didn't go to the house when she recognized Jake's truck. Officially, the Stanwick's garage was no longer a crime scene. All the evidence had been gathered and the department had allowed George to get it cleaned and repaired. But Meg couldn't help being drawn to the garage over and over again. There had to be a clue that had been missed. She even had combed the hill beside the house looking for some clues after Steve told her that Jake saw an animal disappear up the hill. Of course, she found hairs caught in some bushes and a few spatters of blood. They were from an animal and not Kathy.

Meg had an expandable file stuffed with papers on the seat next to her. She kept going over the evidence and still couldn't find the missing piece. She knew that missing piece was somewhere, somehow connected to Kathy Stanwick. Once she was sure that Jake was gone, she shifted the car into gear and drove up the Stanwick driveway. She stopped near the garage door and got out of her car.

As Meg stepped out of the car, she realized she was wearing the same clothes that she had on the day before. She wondered if Mrs. Stanwick would notice. It was late when she decided to call it a night and she didn't feel like driving all the way to Albany. Her fiancé had been so self-involved lately and she didn't want to talk to him. He had left a message on her cell phone complaining about her lack of commitment.

Meg walked past the garage and glanced in a window. She grimaced when she saw the two cars parked in there, feeling like it was destroying her missing evidence. As she walked around the corner of the house toward the front door, she could hear the fighting. She stopped and listened for a moment. At the front door, she could clearly hear Mrs. Stanwick berating her son, whose quiet response Meg couldn't hear. She reached out to ring the doorbell and stopped. She had no real reason for being there and they would know she heard them argue.

Meg turned away from the door and stepped off the porch. She looked around the tree covered yard. All these woods around them and the whole front yard was sheltered by trees. Meg wondered why they didn't just take down some trees and let the front yard be a yard. There was a small pond on the side of the yard near the woods and Meg noticed for the first time a small bench on the one side. She walked over to the pond wondering how she never noticed this before.

The area had been carefully cleared and mulch had been spread around the one side of the pond. There was even a flower bed in back of the bench. Meg looked around the bench and the ground. There was a small clearing in the trees. The early morning sun was able to break through and the pond sparkled with the sunlight. Meg sat down on the bench and looked around. It was a beautiful spot and she just sat in the quiet morning and took it all in.

"Detective Riley?" Meg jumped up and saw George standing behind her. "I thought for a minute that you were Kathy. This is her favorite place."

"I'm so sorry, Mr. Stanwick. I just came by…and…" Meg stumbled around trying to think of an excuse. "I just never noticed this area before."

"Well, stay as long as you like," George said. "Kathy loves coming out here early in the morning. Maybe you'll find what you need here. I'm on my way out for a while. Is there anything you need from me?"

"No, I won't be here long."

"That's fine. If it helps you find my wife, stay as long as you need to. I just want her home."

George turned and walked back toward the house. Meg took a deep nervous breath and turned away. She walked along the mulched side of the pond to where the overgrowth began. On this side, she could look up and see the house and Mrs. Stanwick standing in a large bay window looking at her. Meg looked around as if searching for something. That's when she finally found her missing clue. Caught in one of the branches of a tree was a ripped piece of purple cloth. Meg saw a little blood spatter on the cloth and reached in her pocket. Calling the station for Reggie, Meg also saw footprints in the soft dirt beside the pond heading into the woods.

CHAPTER 18

It was afternoon when Meg finally got in her car to leave the Stanwicks. George had identified the cloth as matching the blouse that Kathy had been wearing the day she disappeared. Reggie and Driscole arrived to gather the forensic evidence. New searchers came to search the area of the woods where the footprints faded into the dense undergrowth. Reggie had called in the state troopers to track with their police dogs. The search so far had revealed nothing aside from the cloth and a few footprints. Driscole took the evidence back to the station.

Although Mrs. Stanwick didn't notice that Meg was wearing the same clothes, Reggie did. He insisted once the search was underway that Meg go home, get cleaned up, and get some rest. Mrs. Stanwick left before Meg, her eyes were red and puffy. Meg didn't want to leave insisting this was the break they had been waiting for, but Reggie took charge and insisted she go home. When Jake showed up with a few men from his church, Meg finally left. She felt left out anyway.

It was a long drive to the condo outside of Albany. Meg sighed thinking about seeing Rick now that she had hardly been home in the past week. Rick thought of her job as an amusing hobby even though he was a lawyer. He kept insisting she transfer to a closer precinct, but her heart was in Granelle. Another thing Rick didn't understand.

As Meg reached the condo, she noticed Rick's Mercedes in its spot and swore under her breath. She had hoped that this early in the day that he would still be at work. She pulled up into her assigned spot and shut off her car. She gathered all her paperwork and glanced in the mirror assessing her appearance. Well, if they were getting married, he'd better get used to her being a bit dirty from time to time.

She climbed the long steps to the front door and felt all the weariness of the past week wash over her. She pulled her keys out and unlocked the door. The smells of cooking hit her and she was suddenly hungry.

"Hey, Rick, I'm home," Meg called out as she slipped her shoes off by the door. She set her keys on a little table that was near the door and put the file of papers next to them. She slipped off her jacket and hung it on a hook.

"Rick?" Meg called out again. She walked through the hallway toward the kitchen. The normally immaculate kitchen had a few dishes in the sink and something cooking in the oven. Meg could hear the sounds of water coming from down the hall. With an uneasy feeling, Meg walked to their bedroom. The sounds of the shower running were clearer from here. Meg went into the bedroom and found the bed unmade and clothes on the floor. She picked up the clothes and looked at them making sure they were Rick's.

Meg tossed the clothes on the bed and went to the door to the bathroom. She quietly opened the door and looked inside. Behind the frosted shower door, Meg could see Rick showering.

"Rick, it's me," Meg said.

"I thought I heard you come in. I'm almost finished," Rick said. Meg stood watching for a few minutes without saying anything. She went back into the bedroom and undressed, dropping her dirty clothes down a laundry chute. She slipped into a robe as she heard the shower shut off and Rick moving around in the bathroom. He came into the bedroom in a towel and went to the closet.

"So what brings you home in the middle of the day," Meg asked. Rick glanced over at her.

"I might ask you the same question. I haven't seen much of you lately," he said defensively.

"My boss sent me home since I did an all nighter."

"Hmp, shouldn't you be beyond doing night shifts?"

"Not when there are still two missing women and another woman dead."

"Ah," Rick said turning back to his closet.

"What's that suppose to mean?"

"I've asked you over and over again to give up this crusade work. But that means more to you than I do, apparently."

"That's not fair. I was a detective when you met me."

"Yes, and you can still be a detective. But one that comes home every once in a while."

"I missed one night."

"One night and how many late nights when I'm already asleep when you come home. I told you that you can get into a closer precinct, but you won't."

"You never answered my question."

"Which one was that?" he said as he began to dress.

"Why are you home? And why are you taking a shower in the middle of the day? Is there something going on that I should know about?"

Rick stopped and looked at her. His face was dark and she could tell he was angry. "Well, detective. I have good reason to be home. My parents are coming over for dinner to bring the list of guests they want to invite to my wedding. My fiancée is supposed to be with me so that we can make plans with my parents for the rehearsal dinner."

Meg's face changed to bewilderment. "That's tonight?" Rick slammed the door to the closet making Meg jump.

"Yes, it's tonight," Rick yelled. "I thought you came home early because you remembered. I thought for one minute that maybe you were back. But I should have figured that you weren't."

"I'm sorry. It's just that there is so much going on with the case…."

"Forget it Meg. I'll just call my parents and tell them not to bother."

"Don't do that. I just need to take a shower. You've already started dinner."

Rick sat down on the edge of the bed in frustration. Meg came over and tried to put her arm around him. He pushed her away roughly.

"No, not this time. It's not this case or even your job and you know it. I'm tired of fighting with you."

"What do you mean?" Meg asked in a quiet voice.

"I'm not Jake Peterson. I can never be him."

"I don't want Jake. I want you."

Rick shook his head. "You were all set to leave Granelle until Jake came back to town. I'm not a fool. I saw how you changed."

"No. You've got it wrong. Martha Rowley disappeared. It's the first real case I've had as a detective."

"Whatever," Rick said standing. He finished buttoning his shirt. "I never wanted to do this. But I'm giving you an ultimatum. I love you and I thought we had something special."

"We still do. Look, your parents will be here soon. Let me get ready. We can talk about this later."

"No," Rick said firmly. "I'm going to stay with Tony tonight. I'll call my parents and excuse us for tonight. I'll give you until tomorrow when I come home from work. Leave Granelle and take the job in Albany. If you are here when I get home, I'll know that you are committed to us and our future."

Meg just stared for a minute. "Let me get this straight. You're breaking up with me?"

"No, I'm giving you that decision. If you don't quit the Granelle police department tomorrow, don't come home."

"Rick, be reasonable. There are two…"

"Stop it Meg. I've given you my decision," Rick said and walked out of the bedroom. Meg followed unsure of what to do. Rick went into the kitchen grabbing his wallet and keys. He picked up the phone and called his parents. Meg stood there staring at him while he talked to his mother. Meg could hear the finality in his voice. She just stood in that same spot for a while after he left.

CHAPTER 19

Meg wandered around the condo for a long time. She looked at pictures of Rick, read notes that he had written to her, and tried to decide what to do. She ate the dinner he had made and cleaned up the kitchen. She was mad that he was making her make this decision, yet she could understand his feelings too. She finally took a long hot shower and got into pajamas.

Finally, she went and took the expandable file with all her case notes in it. She spread everything out onto the kitchen table. Meg went into the bedroom and pulled out her laptop computer. She set that up on the table with her papers. She decided either way, the notes should be put into some order. She spent hours compiling her notes into a word processing program and breaking down the similarities and the differences between the cases.

Meg was finding that there was a connection to some type of animal. She didn't need any more evidence to convince her that they were all connected, even Jake's old cases. But there were many holes too. She knew that Angelos had been convicted on circumstantial evidence. Meg searched for solid evidence that she would tie back to a real person, but knew that she didn't have enough yet.

Meg looked at the clock and was surprised that it was almost 11:00. She felt a stab of guilt as she realized that she spent the past several hours working and hadn't thought about Rick once. She stood up stretching and walked to the fridge to get a cold soda. The phone rang.

"Hello," Meg answered.

"Hope I didn't wake you."

"No, Captain. I was just going over some case notes," Meg said surprised by the call. "Is everything okay? Did you find Stanwick?"

"I just wanted to fill you in. The trail led to a dead end. The dogs tracked a scent through the woods to a road and then it ended. The theory is that whoever kidnapped Kathy Stanwick had a car waiting."

"Oh, I was hoping we would find her."

"You aren't the only one. Now, about what you were doing at the Stanwick house this morning…"

"Captain, I was following a hunch. It paid off, didn't it?"

"Riley," he said cautiously. "Mr. Stanwick told me how he found you sitting in his front lawn this morning. He was very nice about it and all. But then his mother told me how you've been badgering him and coming over all the time."

"I'm investigating," Meg said trying to explain. She pulled the soda out and drank right from the bottle.

"There is a difference between investigating and obsessing. I've seen both and right now, I think your borderline. Investigate the families, but don't badger them. Do you understand me?"

"Yes, captain," she said rolling her eyes. At least it was over the phone.

"I want to see you in my office at 9:00 AM, sharp," Reggie went on. "I want to see what evidence you have so far."

"Okay. I'll see you then."

"Riley," he said roughly. "Don't be late." Reggie hung up before she could reply. She set the phone on the kitchen counter and went back to her laptop. She checked her email and was surprised to find one she had been waiting for. It was from England about some cases she read about on the Internet. She quickly read the note and opened the zip file that was attached. The email told her that Dr. Harry Chevers was teaching a class at a small college in Albany. He was working for the historical society and he had consulted on the cases in England.

Excited, she ran to Rick's office to print off the information to compare the notes to the case she was working on. As the printer began to print the long file, Meg realized that she had made her decision. While the printer continued to work, Meg went into the bedroom and opened the closet. She began to take her clothes out and pile them on the bed. She didn't have a lot to pack, mostly clothes, stuff from the bathroom, and a few knick knacks. Other than that, most of her own furniture had been put into storage when she moved in with Rick.

Sadly, Meg pulled off her engagement ring and put it in the small black velvet box that Rick had given her. She put it on the nightstand on Rick's side of the bed. She went back to the kitchen table and wrote a note to Rick. Hopefully, when this was all over, they could work out their differences. For now, Meg felt she had to find Martha and Kathy. She felt the key to finding them was in the email file that was printing on Rick's computer. First thing in the morning, Meg planned on making an appointment to meet Dr. Chevers to see if he can explain those strange animal hairs.

CHAPTER 20

Jake couldn't figure out why Barbara Higgins had been sitting waiting for him this morning. Mrs. Baxter had her waiting in the conference room and gave Jake one of her disapproving looks as Jake went in to find out what she wanted to talk to him about. A half an hour later, Jake found his thoughts drifting as Barbara was explaining through tears about her problems with her mother. At thirty five, she should be able to go out without telling her mother every move. But her mother made it clear that living at home required Barbara to tell her where she was going and when she would be home. How would she ever meet a man if her mother wouldn't let her go out? Jake couldn't help noticing that Barbara had dressed up to meet with him this morning and that she was wearing a lot of perfume.

Jake had already set boundaries with Barbara and even kept the door opened. But she kept inching closer as she explained how her mother won't let her get her own apartment unless she was married. She had money saved for an apartment. Jake looked at the clock and decided it was time for him to get to other issues.

Finally, Jake said, "You know if you were busy with some things at the church, maybe your mother wouldn't be so protective of you. Why don't you sign up to help at the pot luck dinner for the ladies' auxiliary? I'm sure that's something your mother wouldn't mind you being involved with."

"Oh...I'm not sure. The auxiliary is for older ladies."

"No, we have several younger women involved and it would be a great way for you to make some new friends. Why don't you pray about it? Mrs. Baxter can give you more information about their activities. It's a great way to get involved with the church," Jake said as he stood and went to the door.

"I'll see," Barbara said with a big smile. "Can I get another appointment?"

"Why don't you check with Mrs. Baxter and see if she can find you a time in my schedule next week."

"Don't you think I should come in more than once a week?"

"I think once a week is enough for now. Once Pastor Walt comes back, maybe he can meet with you more frequently," Jake said as he stepped out of the room and began walking toward Mrs. Baxter's desk. Mrs. Baxter looked up with a smile.

"Mrs. Baxter, could you give Barbara some information about the ladies' auxiliary?"

"Of course," said Mrs. Baxter as she pulled out a file from her drawer. Barbara's smile froze in place as she walked over to Mrs. Baxter. As she launched into all the details of the auxiliary, Jake went to his office and closed the door. He pulled out a file and started looking at the proposals to repair the church roof. All the estimates were so different and Jake was trying to figure out what the church really needed. A few minutes later, there was a knock on his door.

"Come on in," Jake called out as he jotted down a few notes.

"Pastor Jake," said Mrs. Baxter as she opened the door. "I don't think Barbara was interested in the auxiliary. Did she tell you she was?"

"No. I suggested it to her. I thought it would be a good way for her to get involved at the church."

"Oh," she said walking over to the desk. "I see you're looking at the proposals. I know that Mr. Kline's bid was a little bit higher, but he's been on our church rolls for years."

"I don't know Mr. Kline...do I?"

"Well, he doesn't really attend. But we give him some special consideration in order to encourage him to come back and fellowship with us."

"So, what's the point of having bids if we give the work to Mr. Kline?"

Mrs. Baxter looked perplexed, "To keep him honest."

Jake sat back in his chair. "Do you realize how that sounds?"

"I don't know what you mean? Anyway, I have the bulletin ready for you to look at and I need to make the copies this afternoon. Can you stop working on the proposals and just okay that for me? And can you also give me your song list for Sunday? It was a little cumbersome having you jumping around a lot last week."

"Okay, I'll get the bulletin right back to you. As far as a song list...I'd rather be led by the Holy Spirit."

"That's not the way we do it, Pastor Jake. It makes things much more difficult for me...."

"Why don't I have one of the teens do the overhead?" Jake offered. "That way they would feel that they are involved. I've gotten to know a bunch of them since I've been here and they are a great group of kids."

"Well, that might be so, but let's not change anything right now. Pastor Walt's been doing things a certain way for a long time."

"We can try it out."

"Look, there are too many other things that you need to concern yourself with. Let's wait and see what Pastor Walt thinks when he comes back," Mrs. Baxter said in a dismissive tone. "I need to step out for lunch today. Just get the bulletin and a song list to me before I leave."

As she left, Jake sighed in frustration and then began to pray. He knew that he couldn't change the bulletin and any song list would be changed anyway. He wondered why she went through the motions.

A buzzer on his phone rang and he picked it up, "Yes, Mrs. Baxter."

"If you sign off on that proposal, I can call Mr. Kline. He told me he has some free time early next week to start the work."

Jake sat and didn't know what to say because he didn't want to offend her. "Hello, Pastor Jake...."

"I heard you. I'm just not sure."

"Oh, that Jessie Buchanan called while you were in your meeting. She asked if you could call her back."

"Thank you," Jake said about to hang up.

"One more thing. The lady's room has a broken hinge on the cabinet. You'll need to fix it before Sunday."

Jake closed his eyes and rubbed his forehead while Mrs. Baxter kept talking. Finally, he told her he needed to get a few things finished. When he hung up, he looked up Jessie's cell phone number and called her back.

"I'm so glad you called me back," Jessie said frantically. "I'm at the court house. But my lawyer never showed up. The judge called my case and asked me what was going on, but I don't know. He said he would call my case later. I don't know what to do."

"Okay, who's your lawyer?"

"I don't know. It is someone who the court appointed."

"Does the clerk know?"

"Who's the clerk?"

"Is Clyde with you?"

"No," she said in a low voice. "He left me."

"I'm sorry, Jessie, I didn't know. I'll come down and walk you through this."

"Thank you so much. I don't mean to be a problem. I just don't want to go to jail."

"It's okay. I'll be right down."

Jake picked up the bulletin and glanced it over. It looked like every other bulletin except for the sermon title. He jotted a few song names on a piece of paper. Then he grabbed his jacket and headed out. He stopped and dropped the papers on Mrs. Baxter's desk.

"Where are you going?" Mrs. Baxter said looking up from her computer.

"One of our members has an emergency," Jake said putting his jacket on.

"Who?" she asked suspiciously. "Not that Jessie Buchanan."

"I'll be back when I'm through," he replied walking to the door.

"Wait," she said standing up. "Did you sign the proposal for the roof?"

Jake stopped with his hand on the door. "No. I need more time to think about this."

"But, the roof is leaking into the closet and Mr. Kline can do the work next week."

"I've got to run. I'll talk to you after lunch," Jake said as he stepped outside. The door closed causing a cold gust of wind to blow in. Mrs. Baxter scrambled to keep a pile of papers from blowing off her desk. Shaking her head, she went back to work.

CHAPTER 21

Jake sat in the hall outside the court room with Jessie. The clerk told Jake that the court appointed lawyer was a new young lawyer that Jake didn't know. After a few phone calls, Jake found him in a meeting. He would come to the courthouse when he was through. So, Jake sat making small talk with Jessie waiting for either the lawyer to show up or the bailiff saying Jessie's case had been recalled.

Jake looked down the hall and saw Reggie coming into the courthouse. Reggie saw Jake and came over. "Peterson," Reggie said and nodded at Jessie. "What brings you here?"

"This is Mrs. Buchanan. She needed some support today," Jake replied.

"Buchanan? Is she the one that assaulted Matthews?"

Jake looked down at Jessie and saw her look away, her eyes filling with tears. He motioned to Reggie to move away. They moved to a small alcove where Jake knew they would not be heard.

"I hardly call what happened assault," Jake said.

"Didn't she hit Matthews with a frying pan? That's what I heard. That's even what your statement said."

"Reggie, Matthews grabbed her to make her go into the kitchen with him. She was holding a frying pan and swung around to break his hold. The pan hit him in the arm."

Reggie peeked around the corner at the little woman sitting on the bench wiping tears from her cheeks. "Humph. She doesn't look like she can hit too hard either."

"Jessie was mad. She was threatening her husband with the pan, but not Matthews."

"You going to vouch for her in court?"

"Yes, I had been counseling them before this incident at my church. The aggression was never on her part. I'm willing to attest to that."

Reggie just looked Jake over. "So, let me get this straight. You're telling me about this woman to help her out of trouble. Right?"

"Where are you going with this, Reggie?"

Reggie shrugged pretending innocence. "I'm just asking…wouldn't what you just told me be consider privileged information?"

Jake hesitated a moment. "It was all in my statement. Where's the privilege?"

"That you were counseling them and she wasn't aggressive. Her husband was though."

"Isn't that common knowledge?"

"Not to me it wasn't."

"Oh," Jake said sheepishly. "I wasn't thinking of it that way."

"Tell you what. We are old friends. Right?"

"I don't think I like where this is going."

Reggie laughed, "You're probably right. You probably aren't going to like this. But I'm willing to work something out with you."

"Look, I realize that Matthews filed the report and that Jessie needs to show respect to the police."

"Now hold on a minute," Reggie said holding up his hand. "Matthews works for me. I'm hearing your side and know that you are a dependable witness. I take it her husband is a witness for the state seeing you are sitting with her instead of him."

Jake nodded. "Sounds that way. They just split up."

"So, the husband is going to throw her in. She's a down and out woman. The judge could go either way on this one."

"What's the angle here?"

"You're willing to push the line on privilege to help out this woman. I'm asking you to do the same thing to help the Stanwicks."

"We already covered this. Besides, I have nothing to offer," Jake said shaking his head.

"This is what I'm offering you. I'll give Mrs. Buchanan a get out of jail free card if you just review the Stanwick case and give me your opinion. I'm not asking you to join the force or do anything apart from looking at the file. Tell me if you think it is possible that this is a copy cat or if this is the real deal."

"You really think these cases are linked to Angelos?"

"You're my expert. Just give me a little time today and I'll drop the charges against her," Reggie said jerking his thumb in Jessie's direction.

"But how do we explain that to Jessie without having Matthews lose his creditability with the public?"

"Easy. I'll drop the charges without prejudice. Meaning if she ever hits a cop again, this will be used against her. I'm giving her a break because she's getting counseling."

"And if I can't help you?"

Reggie shrugged, "Let her take her chances at trial. You know Judge Murphy just as well as I do. What mood is he in today?"

Jake stood weighing his options and then nodded. "I'm doing this for Jessie. But only reviewing the file to see if there are any similarities. I can't be gone too long either or Mrs. Baxter will come hunt me down."

Reggie laughed again. "You mean old Corrine Baxter is still working at that church?"

"Yes, and she wants me in the office all the time."

"Let me go talk to the DA. Stay put and don't tell her anything until I work out the details. I'll be right back."

Jake went back to the bench and sat with Jessie. A few hours later, Jake sat in Reggie's office reading the forensic evidence in the Stanwick case. Meg had the other files and she wasn't in the squad room. Apparently, she was on her way, but Jake told Reggie he had to get back to the church…soon. Mrs. Baxter had called him five times in the last hour.

Reggie was pacing in the squad room and Meg rushed in out of breath. Jake heard Reggie yelling at her for being late as his cell phone rang again. This time Jake turned the phone off and waited. Meg came in with a messy file and sat in the chair opposite Jake. Reggie sank in the chair behind the desk and the chair groaned under his weight.

"Sorry," Meg began. "I was checking out a lead."

"What lead?" Reggie said glaring at her.

"It turned out to be nothing. Again, sorry," she said as she began pulling out a thin folder from her expandable file. "Here are just some of my notes on the Stanwick case. The damaged car, the pictures of the garage. The usual stuff. It's the same file I tried to show you last week."

Jake looked at her as he reached over to take the file from her hand. "Did you look at this file last week?" Reggie asked.

"Just briefly," Jake replied as he opened the folder and looked at the pictures of the scene again. He saw the notes on his old case records too.

"Well," Meg said. "Come up with anything yet?"

Jake looked back at her and saw the hurt and sarcasm in her eyes. He looked back at the pages. "I didn't read this file last week. I left it on the desk. So, I don't have any opinion yet."

"Can I point out a few things to you?"

"No," Jake said reading. "I'd rather form my own opinion."

"Oh, of course," she said.

"Riley," Reggie barked. "Go get me coffee now."

Looking stung, Meg dropped her file on the corner of Reggie's desk with a bang and stormed out.

"Why don't you just take it with you and call me tomorrow. I know it's distracting here. And…" Reggie started.

"No. It's okay. I don't really have time to do much more than I've already given you. I've got a few people to visit and I have to finish Sunday's sermon," Jake said as he continued to read. Reggie sat back and just watched Jake. Jake scanned a few sheets and went back to the forensic folder he reviewed before. Meg came back in and handed Reggie a Styrofoam cup with coffee. She sat down in a huff.

"Well," Jake finally said setting the file and papers down on Reggie's desk. "There are a few things. It looks like Kathy fought. There is her blood in the car and the obvious damage to the car and garage. In the old cases, there was no sign of violence the women were just reported missing. That's the same as Martha Rowley. She just disappeared too."

"What about the scratches?" Meg asked. "Surely you see the forensics don't you?"

"Yeah. I saw the scratches. There were scratches in the horse stall where we found Angelos. And they do have a similar pattern to the scratches on Kathy's car hood. But we don't know what made them."

"What about the hairs?"

"The hairs?" Jake said looking confused.

"Don't you see the animal hairs in the Stanwick car match the hairs on the clothes in the Angelos case?"

"You mentioned that to me at the funeral. We already discussed this."

Meg sighed in frustration and grabbed the file. "Didn't you see the lab report?"

"Riley," Reggie said in a cautious voice. "Where are you going with this?"

Meg looked at Reggie as if realizing he was still there. "I just want Jake to see if he thinks it's significant."

"I don't need to see that. It's not significant. What I think is that the Rowley case has some similarities to Angelos. If I had to guess, I'd say it's probably a copy cat. Someone who read something about the old cases. Kathy's disappearance is too messy to have been the same work."

"And you can't see any significance even after you saw something in the woods that night?"

"I told you, I saw a dog. It ran away when I yelled. When I look at the whole picture, I think that the Rowley case and the Stanwick case are two separate cases. I almost wonder if Kathy caught someone breaking into the house and they attacked her. Maybe they took her to make it look like it was connected to Rowley," Jake said looking up at Reggie and standing up. "Sorry that I couldn't be of more help to you. I've really got to get back to the church."

Reggie and Meg stood too. Meg began to gather the paperwork and put it back in her file. "I appreciate you taking the time. Wish you could help out more. Riley, sit. We aren't finished."

Jake walked out and closed the door behind him. He could hear the heated discussion as he left the station to go back to the church. He took out his cell phone to call the church and saw that Mrs. Baxter had called him three more times.

CHAPTER 22

Trevor walked to the back of the rented house. He was surprised to see so much activity at the Craigs' house when he drove past a few minutes before. A large rental truck was in the driveway and people were filling it up with boxes. He saw sparks drift in the air as he walked around the corner of the house. Shamus poked at a fire with a long stick. The creature lay near the fire staring into the hot red embers.

"Shamus," Trevor said approaching the man. "Have you heard anything today about the Craigs?"

"Nay," the old man said in his Irish brogue. His dirty work pants and old plaid shirt fit him tightly. His thick white hair hung in his face. As he turned, Trevor noticed how ruddy his cheeks were.

"You don't look well. Did you take your medication today?" Trevor asked with concern.

"Aye. Just the work. I'm getting older."

Trevor grunted and walked over the creature. He knelt next to her and began to pet her. She growled low in her throat. "How is she?" Trevor asked.

"She's hurting. Just wants to lie outside and watch."

"And him?"

Shamus looked toward the woods and pointed. "Out there somewhere. Probably hunting."

"With all the searchers. Maybe we should just keep them inside for now. We are so close. I'd hate to have something happen to ruin things now."

"She will probably stay, but not him. How's the plan going?"

"Good. I will get the next one soon. The last one didn't go so well so I think I should wait a few days until things settle back down again. But I'm worried about the boy."

"Why?" Shamus poked the fire again sending up another shower of sparks.

"There is a for sale sign in front of the house and it looks like they are packing up."

Shamus looked concerned. "That's not good. Maybe we should take the boy now."

Trevor stood up and brushed dry leaves from his pants. "I can't. It has to be right for it to work."

"What are you going to do then? If we lose the boy…"

"We won't." Trevor said. "After all these years, why can't you trust me to do it right?"

"Because of before."

"That wasn't my fault."

"Nay? You refused to listen. It needed to be a child. Like you were."

"I know that now. That's why I picked Sam."

"And you will lose him."

"No, I won't. It will work this time."

Trevor stormed away angrily. He went back to the car and got in. He slammed the door and threw the car into drive. The wheels spun out on the dirt driveway. Finally getting traction the car pulled out onto the dirt road. The drive back down the road to the Craigs didn't give Trevor a long time to ponder what he was doing. But he needed to know what was going on. He pulled up off the road onto the Craig's lawn. He sat for a few minutes looking around. Then Trevor saw the dark shadow in the woods near the detached garage. He knew it was the other creature watching the house.

Trevor got out of the car and the creature watched him. A group of teens came out the side door with boxes. A few were laughing about something. Trevor walked up to the group and smiled. He recognized Karen and approached her.

"Hi Karen. I couldn't help noticing you were packing and thought I'd stop and see if I could help," he said. Karen fumbled with her box and blushed. Trevor smiled recognizing her attraction to him.

"Oh, Mr. Grant," she stuttered. "My dad is in the kitchen. I don't think we need any more help today."

"Thank you. I'll find him." Trevor walked inside and heard another girl whispering to Karen.

"Who's that?"

"My neighbor. Isn't he cute?" Karen whispered back. Trevor found Stanley sitting in the kitchen. Boxes were everywhere and everything was in disarray. Pots and pans, dishes, silverware covered every spot on the counter.

"Stanley," Trevor said. "I can't help noticing all the activity."

Stanley looked up and nodded wearily. "It's been a long week."

"Anything I can do to help?"

"I don't think so. We're just about done for the day."

"It looks like there is still so much to do," Trevor said looking around the kitchen. Stanley looked around too and nodded.

"Yes there is still so much to do. But it doesn't all have to be done today. Just Karen's stuff."

"Karen?"

"She's going to go down and stay with my sister for now. It's been so rough on her losing her mother. Sam and I are going to stay for a little while longer."

"Well, if there is anything I can do to help, please let me know. After all we are neighbors."

"Sure," Stanley said distracted. Then he seemed to remember something. "I do have a question for you. Have you seen any wild animals around here lately? I thought I heard something the other night and I'm concerned about letting Sam be outside alone."

"Wild animal? I don't think so. What do you think it was?"

"I'm not sure. Maybe a wolf or something?"

Trevor shrugged. "No, I haven't seen anything. I live deeper in the woods than you. Must have just been a dog or something. Maybe even my dog."

"You have a dog? Sam didn't mention that?"

"No," Trevor smiled. "He didn't meet my dog yet."

"Oh," Stanley said with some uncertainty. "Well, better get this kitchen straightened up a bit. My sister is trying to do a lot for me before she leaves tomorrow."

"Again, call me if I can help."

Trevor turned and left. He even flirted a little with Karen's friend making her giggle. As he walked back to his car, he noticed the creature was still there. As he turned the car around and drove back to the house, it followed in the woods staying in the shadows.

CHAPTER 23

Meg sat at her desk reading through the reports on the evidence gathered at the Stanwicks the day before. The report indicated that due to the depth of the prints, that the person either was very heavy or carrying someone heavy. Meg figured that was the person who carried Kathy Stanwick away after her assault in the garage. She looked in the report and through the pictures hoping for some picture of animal prints, but there were none. She even sat with a magnifying glass trying to find something in the pictures that just wasn't there. There were no traces of the animal hairs either.

Reggie had given her the reports in his office after Jake left. The lack of evidence about an animal being in the new area had Reggie agreeing with Jake that it was not important. Frustrated, Meg tried to explain about the email from London, but Reggie just told her to stop wasting time.

As she thought about the footprints, Meg began to wonder why this hadn't been found within days of Kathy's disappearance. Not only had her squad been out at the scene, but state troopers had come out to aid in the search. The footprints were so obvious when she found them that she hadn't thought about that yesterday. She was excited about finding any clue. Meg got up and grabbed her coat. She needed to go back and look again.

Driving out to the Stanwicks, Meg thought what Reggie had said about badgering the families. Hopefully, George would understand. It was getting late in the day and Meg was still driving around with her stuff in the car too. Eventually, she knew she'd have to find a place to sleep for the night, but at least it would be in Granelle not an hour's drive away.

As she drove up the Stanwick's driveway, she saw that the lights were already on in the house. Dusk was falling and Meg didn't think she'd find too much this late in the day. She parked in front of the garage doors and looked down to the pond to see the police tape still up. She got out and walked up to the front door.

George was standing in the doorway waiting for her. "Good afternoon, detective. I was beginning to wonder if you forgot about me today."

"No, but I am sorry to come back up again. I was going over some reports today and it struck me how fresh those footprints looked."

"What do you mean?"

"When people were searching for your wife, didn't someone go down by the pond and look all over your front yard too?"

George stepped out of the doorway and stood by Meg looking down at the pond. Meg looked down too. "I don't really know. That night was so hectic. I barely remember what I did."

"I can't help thinking about it. Your wife was the second women to disappear. So, I know that we were really thorough that night. I remember a lot of people searched the woods in back of your house. But we had to have searched down there too."

"You don't think that these are footprints from that night," George stated looking down at Meg.

"No, if they were, there would have been footprints coming and going. Do you mind if I look again? I'm sorry it seems like I keep bothering you."

"I don't mind if it means you'll find my wife, Detective."

Meg started walking down the hill and then turned back around and looked toward the house. George was still standing there looking back at her. "Mr. Stanwick, what is that way?" Meg asked pointing in the opposite direction of the footprints.

George looked to his right toward where she was pointing. "Directly through those woods are the railroad tracks and beyond that is Dunning Road."

Meg stood looking toward the opposite woods and then started going in that direction. "What are you doing?" George asked.

"I was just thinking that if someone purposely came back to draw our attention to the woods near the pond. Why?"

"Do you mind if I come with you?" George asked.

"It's getting dark. I don't even know what I'll find. Why don't you just wait here?"

"I'll grab a flashlight. I'm tired of sitting around while Kathy is gone."

Meg nodded and kept walking back toward the driveway toward the other woods. George came running up behind her with a flashlight he got from the house. Together they looked around the edge of the property. There was an opening that looked like a pathway into the woods. Meg headed into the woods with George following behind. It was gloomy in the dense interior of the woods. The flashlight made a small ring of light in front of Meg's feet.

"Mr. Stanwick?"

"Please call me George."

"Okay. Did you ever notice kids in the woods a lot or using your yard as a shortcut?"

"Not really, but I was never home very often. I worked a lot of hours."

"Huh. It looked like this was a fairly new path."

They kept walking through the woods and came to the railroad bed. Meg stood on the tracks looked up and down them. Dense woods hemmed in the tracks on both sides. Meg hoped to see another path on the other side.

"So, it leads to a dead end," George said looking around too.

"Not necessarily. Which way would the tracks cross over a road?"

"I think probably that way," George said pointing right down the track. Meg stepped onto the track heading right with George following. About hundred feet down, there was a dark path opening on the opposite side. Meg looked back at George and stepped off the track and down the slope into the dark woods again. They followed the path deeper into the woods. The path wound through the woods and finally, they found themselves coming to a clearing. Meg stopped just inside the woods and George came along side her. There was an old dilapidated house with a dim light inside. The path ended in a backyard.

"Do you recognize this house?" Meg asked whispering.

"No."

"I do. It belonged to old man Hanson. He passed away about five years ago. The house was in such disrepair that the family couldn't sell it. But someone's been renting it, from what I've heard."

They stood quietly looking at the house and an old man came out of the back door. The hinges on the old screen door screeched in protest and then slammed back into the door frame when he let go. George shut the flashlight off and they quietly stood watching the man. He stopped and stared for a moment right where they were standing, then walked to a shed. He came out a few minutes later with a burlap bag and went back into the house.

Meg motioned George to go back up the embankment toward the railroad tracks. In the darkness on the porch, a dark shadow watched them. Sensing something, George looked back to the house. But the figure was just part of a dark shadow. He nudged Meg and whispered. She stopped and looked at the porch too. Shaking her head, she started back up the hill. At the top of the embankment, Meg pulled out a small notebook. Using the glow from George's flashlight she made a note to see who rented the house.

They walked further down the tracks and found another path. Meg followed it down until she was in the woods in back of the Craig's house. She stood looking around the yard. Not seeing anything out of the ordinary, they took the path back toward George's house. A chill was settling in and Meg was getting cold. When George offered to make some coffee, Meg declined knowing she would need to figure out where to spend the night.

CHAPTER 24

The dark shadow watched until the pair disappeared into the woods. He then went into the house and found the old man.

"Did you see the people in the woods?" Trevor asked.

"Aye," Shamus said pulling out some old tools from the burlap bag.

"Who do you think it was?"

"That was the police. They are looking for your last victim," Shamus said and he sat down hard on a kitchen chair.

Trevor made a disgusted noise, "You can't know that. It was dark."

"Aye, but I can. I know the woman, Riley is her name."

"It was dark. You can't know...."

Shamus cut him off. "Don't argue with me boy. You've made many mistakes with that Stanwick woman. You need to get rid of her."

"No, we are too close."

"Nay, we are a long way. You need to get rid of her. She's wrong for the ceremony and she prays."

Trevor laughed. "I don't care about her prayers."

"Did I not teach you anything? I feel the power of those prayers through the darkness. Many are praying for her and that will lead people here. You need to get rid of her tonight if we are to have any peace. Then go back to the plan."

"I'm the keeper. I will do what I think is best."

The two men stared at each other for a moment, challenging each other. Trevor turned away and slammed his fist on the counter.

"It is as I thought," Shamus said. "You are not strong enough. I will need to continue on."

"No," Trevor said quietly. "It is my time to be the keeper. I have waited all these years. We just need to move faster so that we get the boy before his father moves away."

"Maybe we should cut our losses and move on. There are more towns."

"No," Trevor said turning around. "Besides you know she cannot be moved right now."

"Tis true. She is gravely ill."

Fear coursed through Trevor. "But she will get well. I'll see to that."

"We will do what we need to for her and then move on."

Trevor watched Shamus setting the old tools on the table. He would not give up now, not when he felt they were so close. Trevor left the house and got into his car. He drove into town and pulled into a parking lot. He didn't care what Shamus said, he would keep the plan and just move faster to make the boy one of them. He watched people walk down Main Street as he looked for the right victim. He wished it was the weekend so that he would blend in with a crowd since there weren't too many people out.

Trevor heard loud music coming from the local bar and got out of the car. He headed to the side street and walked in. The dimly lit sports bar was about half full. Trevor walked in and squinted in the smoke filled room. As his eyes adjusted to the dim lighting, he noticed two young girls at the end of the bar. He didn't think they were legally able to drink, but they each had a half full mug of beer in front of them. Trevor sat at the bar closer to their end.

"What can I get you," the bartender asked Trevor as she put a coaster in front of him.

"Just a coke." Trevor pulled money out of his pocket and put it on the bar.

The bartender set the drink down and took the money, then wandered back to the other end of the bar. The two girls whispered and were watching Trevor. Trevor glanced over at them as he took a drink. He reached inside his pocket and pulled out a pack of thin cigars. He took one out and felt in his pocket for his lighter.

"Can I offer you a light?" the younger of the two girls asked holding up her lighter.

"Sure, thanks," Trevor smiled as she walked over to him. She held the lighter for him. He cupped his hand over hers as he leaned in to light the cigar. He felt her hand tremble under his and knew he had her. She sat on the bar stool next to him. Trevor glanced over at her friend and realized she had discreetly gone to the ladies' room.

"I'm Trevor and you are?"

"Lauren."

"It's a pleasure to meet you." Trevor took a long drag on his cigar and blew the smoke above Lauren's head. He locked his eyes on hers and smiled.

CHAPTER 25

It was late when Meg settled in at the old Granelle Motel. She brought a suitcase and her case file in with her and left everything else in the car. Meg sat on the old sagging bed propped up on the pillows trying to go over the clues again. But exhaustion from the past week settled in and Meg woke up as the early morning sun poured in the dirty window. She groaned as she moved realizing that not only had she slept in her clothes, but she had slept sitting up against the headboard. As she swung her feet off the bed, her cell phone rang.

Glancing at the clock, Meg realized she was late for work. "Hello," she said as she fumbled with the phone.

"Meg, just what do you think you are doing? And where are you?"

"Good morning to you too, Mom," Meg said pulling her suitcase up on the bed.

"How could you have left Rick?"

"I didn't really leave. We had an argument about my job. That's all."

"I called there and talked to Rick myself. You should have called me."

"Why? There is nothing to tell you. Rick needed some space, so I'm giving it to him. We'll work it out."

"It didn't sound that way to me."

"Look, I'm late for work. I'll call you back later. Maybe we can go out for dinner tonight or something. Okay?"

"You better call. You always say you will and then you don't," her mother wined.

"I'll call. I've really got to run. Bye Mom."

Meg pulled out a change of clothes and threw them on. Running her brush quickly through her hair, she put it in a ponytail. She grabbed her file and quickly left. Meg drove down Main Street and slipped her car into a spot. She walked into the local real estate office.

The receptionist looked up expectantly. Meg pulled out her badge. "I'm Det. Riley. I need to talk to Maureen Reynolds."

The receptionist nodded and made a quick phone call. Meg recognized Maureen when she stepped out of her office. Dressed impeccable in a dark business suit with gold rings and dangly bracelets, Maureen looked like an executive of a Fortune 500 company, instead of a small real estate agent in a small town.

Maureen smiled warmly at Meg and invited her into her office. She told the receptionist to bring them coffee and hold her calls.

As they settled into the chairs, Maureen smiled again, "Finally finding time to visit an old friend or is this official?"

"As much as I would like to just visit with you Mo, I'm here as a detective."

"No one calls me Mo anymore," Maureen said grimacing. The receptionist knocked on the door and brought in a tray of steaming cups of coffee. She set it on the desk and left. Maureen offered a cup to Meg who happily accepted it taking a long drink.

"Okay," Meg said setting the cup down. "I'm trying to track down the name of the person who rented the old Hanson place on Dunning Road."

"I rented that place," Maureen said turning to her computer. "I sure wish the Hanson's would consider putting a little money into the place. No one wants to buy it. It would be really cute too. Maybe a starter home for a newlywed."

Meg cleared her throat. "I'm not looking to buy a house right now. I just want to know who rented it."

"It's a shame you living all the way down in Albany. We don't get to do anything together anymore," she said with a pout. Meg ignored the comment and sat waiting. When she didn't respond, Maureen glanced over. "What's wrong? Domestic bliss not what you thought it would be?"

"I'm here for the name, Mo," Meg said trying to hurry her along.

"Megan Riley, I was your best friend in high school. I can tell when something is wrong. So spill it," Maureen said pulling her chair back over to the desk.

Meg sighed, knowing she wouldn't get any information until she told Maureen something. "It's nothing. Rick and I had a little spat. But, we'll be fine."

"Oh no," Maureen said dramatically. "Give me the gory details."

"Mo, I have to get to the station. Can you give me the name and maybe we can go out to dinner one night and catch up?"

"You always say we'll get together and then we never do."

"Okay, today. We'll do lunch today. Meet me at Joe's Steakhouse around noon."

"Sounds great," Maureen said with a big smile.

"So, the name," Meg said standing.

"At noon."

"What?"

"I'll give you the name when we meet at noon. That way I know you'll show up," Maureen said turning back to her computer monitor with a big smile.

"You're hampering a police investigation," Meg said exasperated.

Maureen laughed. "Not really. I shouldn't even give you that information without a warrant. Confidentiality and all."

"Mo…"

"See you at noon."

"Okay, but I expect more than a name. I want as much info on that old guy as you can give me." Maureen kept working ignoring Meg who finally gave up and left.

Meg arrived at the station over an hour late. The station was busy with a lot of people, including the state police. Meg finally found Pete and asked him what was going on.

"What's going on? Besides two missing women?" Pete said sarcastically.

"I know we have two missing women. I mean…what are all these people doing here this morning?"

Pete just looked her over. "The same thing we've been doing every day, trying to find them. If you had been here for our debriefing, you would know that though."

"I'm the lead investigator. You don't need to talk to me in that tone."

"It's better than the tone you're going to get from Bennett."

Meg started to say something else and then turned and left. She went to her desk and turned on her computer. She slumped down in the chair and heard Reggie's voice coming from the break room. Checking her email, she saw one from Harry Chevers. Excited, she read that he set aside time to talk with her early next week. She emailed him back asking if they could meet sooner.

A dark shadow fell over her desk as Meg hit the send button. She looked up to see Reggie glaring down at her.

"My office," he said walking away.

"I'm sorry I'm late, Captain," she began carefully closing the door behind her. "But I was following up on a lead...."

"Which lead was that?" he said in a low voice.

"Well, when I left last night I stopped at the Stanwicks. I thought about those footprints showing up a week after she disappeared...."

"Tell me something I don't know."

Meg looked confused. "I don't understand."

"I already know what you did last night since Mr. Stanwick was here before I got to work. He told me all about your adventures into the woods last night."

"So, you know that I found these paths...."

"Where should I begin...I guess I'll start with how inappropriate you are being in how you are handling Mr. Stanwick."

"Inappropriate?"

"I told you about badgering him."

"He asked to go with me."

"A suspect wanted to go with you while you investigated a possible lead."

"We eliminated him as a suspect."

"We? Or you? I don't recall ever saying he wasn't still a suspect or at least a person of interest. Let's move on. You know how I feel about punctuality."

"I stopped to follow up on a lead," Meg said quietly.

"Another lead on your strange dog hair?"

"No," Meg said sitting up straighter. "It was a concrete lead."

Reggie sat back in his chair. "I don't have a lot of options right now Riley. You have the potential to be a good investigator. But maybe this case it too big for you."

"I have leads Captain. I just need..."

"I'm giving you enough rope to hang yourself. I need to get searchers back out into the woods again. With the new evidence, the state police are helping in the search. My focus needs to be in the search and rescue. So, you can have a few more days to bring me something concrete. Find a person, Riley. I'll give you two days. You report to me on Thursday morning at 9:00 and show me what you have."

"Yes, sir," Meg said standing.

"Riley, don't be late."

CHAPTER 26

Meg walked into Joe's a little before noon. She glanced around at the tables, but didn't see Maureen yet. She asked for a table and was lead to one in the back corner. Now, she hoped that Maureen wouldn't be late. She had a lot of work to do and couldn't waste any more time. While she waited, she looked over the menu.

"Hi Meg," Maureen said breathlessly as she sat down.

"Okay, spill it," Meg said.

"Not even a hello. Besides, I want to make sure you don't run off. I want to find out all about Rick."

"Mo, I don't have time to play games. I got in a lot of trouble this morning for being late and then didn't even have anything to tell my boss."

Maureen pouted. "I didn't want to get you in trouble. I just want to get caught up with you. It's been months since you've called, and then when you do, it's all business."

"I'm sorry. It's hard living so far away," Meg said lamely. She tried to come up with something to get the information fast. The waitress came over and asked if they were ready to order. Meg ordered fast, but Maureen said she needed more time.

As the waitress walked away, Meg said, "Okay, you win. I don't have a lot of time right now. The captain is giving me less than two days to come up with something. I really need that information so I can find out something about that man, which may just be another dead end."

"I thought we could talk for a bit," she replied without giving in.

"I was going to wait until this case is solved before I said anything about Rick, but I'll tell you if you promise not to get all dramatic."

"Okay, what's up?"

"Rick and I called off the wedding the other day. He thinks my job is more important than him. I stayed at the motel last night."

"Why didn't you call me? You could have stayed with me last night."

"I can't be distracted right now. I have to get the name of that person."

"Okay, okay. But promise me you'll let me help you find a place to live."

"I promise."

Maureen looked satisfied as she reached into her purse. She pulled out a small note pad. "So what kind of a place would you want? An apartment or a house?"

"I just want the information about the Dunning Road house."

"Well, I have to start looking around to find you a place. You can't live in the motel for long. I can see what's available, and then we can go looking."

Meg sighed. "I guess a month to month rental for now. I don't want to make any long-term commitments. I'm pretty sure Rick and I will work things out."

"Okay," Maureen said jotting a few notes down. "But in Granelle that's hard to come by. You don't want to look at Saratoga?"

"No, just something in town."

"Shamus O'Leary."

"What?"

Maureen looked up from her pad. "The old man is Shamus O'Leary. He's from a little town near Dublin in Ireland. He travels a lot, mostly between London and America though."

Meg pulled out her own pad and wrote the information down. "What's he doing in town?"

"He came for track season. Said he doesn't like to stay in Saratoga because it's too busy."

"But track season ended two months ago. Why is he still here?"

"You'd have to ask him. I try not to pry into people's lives."

Meg laughed, "Yeah, sure you don't."

Maureen tried to look all innocent. "Just because people like to talk to me doesn't mean I'm prying."

"I've got to ask…does this O'Leary have a dog?"

Maureen squinted, thinking. "I think there was something. He stayed there before, several years ago, and the owners complained about a dog smell in the house. But then their grandfather had an old coon hound before he passed."

"Do you mind if I pass on lunch?" Meg asked. "I'm not really hungry and I have to follow up on this guy."

"See, I knew you wouldn't stay! I should have waited until the food came," Maureen said. When Meg started to say something, Maureen waved her off. "Go ahead, save the world. You're lucky I like what you ordered."

Meg stood and pulled money out of her pocket. "At least let me pay for lunch."

"You'd better. Oh, give me your cell number. I'll call you later with a few listings."

Meg gave her the number and then left. She looked down at her note pad as she walked to the car and practically ran into someone. Mumbling her apology, she walked around him and went to her car. Standing on the sidewalk watching her, Jake couldn't believe the disheveled person who ran into him was Meg. He watched her drive down the road until her car disappeared around a corner.

Jake headed down the sidewalk past Joe's to a small pizza shop. He knew he had to be back to the church by 1:00 when Mrs. Baxter got back from her lunch break. For now, Jake just wanted a few minutes to be alone. The heat from the pizza ovens hit him and the smell of cooking pizza wafted through the air. Jake realized how hungry he was as he ordered a few slices of pizza and a soda. He took a booth in the far back of the little shop hoping no one would see him.

After a brief prayer of thanks for the food, Jake began to eat. He thought through the past few weeks. He was glad that Jessie had moved in with her family over in Ballston Lake now that the charges had been dropped. But so many other issues continued to bother him.

He thought about George and prayed again for Kathy's safe return. He had been over many times to visit George and was a little unsettled by how George talked about the way Meg was handling Kathy's case. Jake had been at George's a few days ago when Meg had found the footprints. Jake looked at them and knew they had been planted to mislead the investigation. Jake didn't bring his concerns to Reggie though. This additional evidence revitalized the search efforts and Jake hoped that Kathy would be found. Jake wanted to be there today, but so many other issues kept him at the church.

Jake had also been to the Craig's numerous times. He tried to reach out to Sam only to see the boy withdrawal from everyone. Jake knew Sam blamed himself for his mother's death and it bothered Jake. He tried to give Sam some counsel, but the grief made it difficult to reach him. Stanley also blamed himself and Jake felt unprepared to help him either. Jake left each time praying for their grief and hoping that the move to Poughkeepsie would offer them some solace.

Jake worried about how slowly Pastor Walt was healing from his surgery. He was weak and had been moved to another floor of the hospital for physical therapy. He went to Albany several times a week to visit the Ryersons. They always asked about the church and the families and Jake kept reassuring them. More than once, Jake felt Pastor Walt knew the truth about how inadequate Jake was to really lead the church. But those words were left unspoken.

Then there were the problems with the roofing contractor Mrs. Baxter had insisted Jake needed to hire. The work had hardly begun when Mr. Kline had already added to the work and was charging the church double the original quote. Now, he was left explaining to the church board why this contractor had been hired when others had lower quotes. A few of the elders told him that he shouldn't have made that decision without consulting them. When he looked at Mrs. Baxter, she looked away.

Between the counseling, the paperwork, and the other problems that Jake dealt with each day, Jake found little time to prepare for his sermons and devotionals he needed to give. Mrs. Baxter told him that was because he wasted too much time outside of the office visiting the Craigs and George. But Jake felt that was important too.

Jake had long finished his pizza and sat lost in thought. He found himself praying for those people that came to mind. He knew that many of the people in the church were praying too. Time slipped away as Jake continued his prayers for his little town and for direction in his own life. Finally, Jake realized he sat alone in the pizza shop. The lunch hour had quickly flown by and it was close to 2:00. He quickly threw out his garbage and began the walk back to the church on the edge of town.

CHAPTER 27

Meg could find no criminal record on Shamus O'Leary. There was no mention of him in international records either. There was no new evidence anywhere. The footprints were a dead end. Meg just wished she had realized that the footprints were planted that day when the captain was over at the Stanwicks. If she had found the paths when Reggie had been there, he would have seen the connection. With Pete off in a different direction, Meg didn't even have a partner to talk things out with. The only hope she felt she had was finding out what Harry Chevers knew about the mythical creatures that she read about. Maybe she could find a link…maybe. Even her theory about the hairs being a link didn't seem viable to her right then.

Meg drove aimlessly around town. She knew that she couldn't go back to the Rowley or Stanwick houses again. Even her idea that somehow, Mrs. Craig's death was connected had been shot down by the Captain. She could see the searchers in the woods and knew that their search was winding down again. It would be left to the locals again once the state police left at the end of the day. Meg felt left out and isolated. She had never felt that before in her work. There was so much pressure to find Martha and Kathy, but there was no evidence that made sense.

Finally Meg found herself back at the motel. She had agreed to meet Maureen in less than an hour to see a listing for a two-bedroom house that had a month to month option. Meg only gave in because she thought maybe Maureen would remember something else. Meg dropped her case file on the small table next to her laptop. She glanced in a mirror and sighed. Her clothes were still in the suitcases that were by the door. She shrugged figuring it didn't matter anyway.

Meg pulled one of the suitcases over to the bed and opened it. She pulled out a pair of wrinkled jeans and a sweater and got dressed. Her cell phone rang, startling her. Meg dug in her purse and pulled it out as it rang the third time. She held it until it stopped ringing.

Meg pushed the off button and threw the phone on the bed. She pulled her keys out and slipped her shoes on. She paused as she passed a mirror. She stared at the stranger who was looking at her. There were dark circles under her eyes, her face was white, and her hair still in disarray, even after brushing it. Meg didn't look like Meg even to herself. But she didn't care right now.

Meg had already decided just to take the house that Maureen found even though she hadn't seen it yet. She didn't have the time or the patience to look for anything else. As Meg pulled up in front of the house, she moaned at the site of the house. Maureen was already there and had the house opened up.

"Here it is," Maureen gushed as Meg walked up the sidewalk to the house. "I know it isn't much to look at, but it has possibilities."

"I thought you were trying to do me a favor. You really rent places that look like this?"

"Meg, I told you that it was hard to find any month to months in Granelle. This is the only one available. Just look, I'll show you things you can do."

Meg walked through the house while Maureen showed her how it could be fixed up. The dirt and grime could easily be cleaned, some new curtains, the old furniture could be replaced. Once they walked through, Maureen looked at Meg expectantly.

"I suppose what you said is true. I just don't have the time to do any of those things," Meg said shaking her head.

"Well, you can't stay at the motel forever. That would get expensive. Besides, this place is cheap because of the shape it's in."

"Did I tell you that I was living in a brand new condo with Rick?"

"I guess I can keep looking or talk to a few of my clients to see if they would be willing to consider a monthly," she said doubtful.

"See what you can do. I'll think about it."

Maureen smiled. "This could work out well for you. Why don't we have dinner and talk. After all, you blew me off at lunch."

"I can't. I have the same problem that I had at lunch. By the way, is there anything else about O'Leary that you can remember?"

"I did go back and checked the rental agreement. The Hansons definitely said no dogs allowed. So, I guess that's out. He is renting a pretty nice car though. So, I can't figure why he would want that old place if he has enough money to afford that rental."

"What was he driving?"

"It was foreign. A black sleek looking car. I'm not good with cars."

"I'll check it out. Thanks. I'll call you about the house."

Leaving Maureen to lock up the house, Meg walked back to her car and drove off. Meg hated to take it, but unless Maureen found something else, she'd probably be moving in by the end of the week. Forgetting about her mother, Meg drove over to Main Street and decided to have an early dinner since she never did get lunch. She decided to avoid the station, unless Reggie called for her.

Meg found a parking spot in the small parking lot next to Joe's. Walking into the restaurant, Meg was greeted by the hostess.

"Just one today?"

"Yes, but I think I'll just sit at the bar."

"Okay."

Meg walked to the bar and found an opened stool partway down.

"Meg, where have you been hiding yourself these days?" the bartender asked as she mixed a drink.

"I've been living down in Albany, Brenda. But I'm moving back up. Miss the old stomping grounds."

Brenda set the drink down on the bar and walked over to Meg. She handed her a menu. "How's Jake?"

"Jake? Oh, we broke up a few years ago."

"Oh, too bad. I always thought you two were meant for each other."

"Nope. Not us. We're not even partners at work anymore. You know, I think I'll just have a roast beef sandwich and a diet coke."

Brenda took the order to the kitchen and Meg looked around to see if she recognized anyone. In spite of the circumstances, it felt good to be back in Granelle instead of rushing back to Albany every day. Maybe she hadn't made such a huge mess of everything in her life, she thought as Brenda put her drink down. And if Reggie didn't trust her instincts anymore, maybe she ought to transfer to the Saratoga barracks. It was just a short drive to the city.

Meg took the lemon out of her soda and took a drink. She noticed someone watching her, but didn't want to meet his eye. Instead she played with her straw in her drink until her meal came out. Meg didn't realize how hungry she was until she got her food. She couldn't even remember the last real meal she had eaten. As she took her first bite, she looked up and met the eyes of the stranger who had been watching her. Brenda came over and asked how the meal was.

"Good," Meg said as she swallowed.

"I noticed Mr. Grant watching you. Isn't he a doll?" Brenda whispered leaning closer to Meg.

Meg nodded. "You know him?"

"Sort of. He's been coming in since the end of track season. I think he relocated here. He's one of those real charmers. Real smooth with the ladies."

"Did you date him?"

"Me? Nah. I'm not his type. You on the other hand…" She smiled at Meg. "Just watch your heart. I haven't seen him with anyone steady. Just this old guy that he said was his uncle."

"Well, I'm not looking right now. I just broke up with someone," Meg said.

Brenda set Meg's check down on the bar and went on to wait on someone else. Meg felt herself being watched but didn't look up again. Instead she let her thoughts wonder back to the case. As she finished her meal, someone sat down next to her.

"Excuse me." Meg looked up to see Mr. Grant sitting next to her. "Can I buy you a drink?"

"I'm sorry, but I'm not drinking anything but soda right now."

"Trevor Grant," he said smiling as he stuck his hand out.

Automatically, Meg shook his hand. "Meg Riley."

"It's a pleasure to meet you, Ms. Riley."

"Mr. Grant…"

"Please call me Trevor."

"Okay, Trevor. I need to be going. I've got to get back to work." Meg motioned to Brenda and paid her for the meal. Trevor sat watching her. As she stood to leave, Trevor stood too. Meg raised her eyebrows in surprise.

"I was just leaving also. May I walk you out?"

Meg shrugged, "Suit yourself."

As they walked to the car, Trevor tried to make small talk, which Meg ignored. At the car, she stopped and turned to him. "Where are you staying in town? I don't believe I've seen you before."

Trevor smiled. "I'm renting a house on the outskirts of town. Say, aren't you that detective that has been in the news lately?"

Meg hesitated, "Yes, I am."

"It's such a shame about those women. I've been helping in the search."

"Where did you say you were from?"

"I'm from France."

"And you're in Granelle…Why?"

"Perhaps if you want to know more about me, we could have dinner and get to know each other better."

"That sounds interesting. You can call me if you want." Meg reached in her purse and began pulling out one of her business cards and then let it go. "I'm sorry but I haven't got anything to write on. Wait I may have something in my car."

Meg unlocked her car and sat down. She reached into the glove box and found an old envelope. Tearing off a corner, she wrote her cell phone number on it and handed it to Trevor.

"I really do need to get going. Give me a call if you are still interested." Meg closed the door and started the car.

Trevor stepped back and looked down at the number on the paper. He folded it and stuck it in his pocket. Turning he walked back up to Main Street. Meg sat in the car and watched until Trevor disappeared around the front of Joe's. Then she shut her car off and got out. She walked up to Main Street and peaked around the building. She watched Trevor as he weaved his way down the street and get into an expense black car. Meg watched him drive off and then went into Joe's.

Meg went back to the bar and motioned to Brenda. "Hey, I thought you left with Mr. Grant."

"I sort of did. What do you know about him?"

"Not much. He comes in pretty regularly. He loves his steak rare and likes foreign wines. I guess he's from overseas somewhere."

"Do you know where?"

"No. Like I told you before, I'm not his type."

"What is his type? Me?"

"Yeah. He goes for a few types that I've seen. Mostly lonely alone women. You know like you came in alone and looked around. Looking lonely. And attractive too. He doesn't seem to have a preference on age though or wealth."

"Why not you if he seems to not have a preference?"

"I'm attached. My boyfriend comes in and hangs out. I'm unavailable."

"Do you know any of the women he's picked up?"

"No."

"Would you recognize them if I showed you a few pictures?"

"Sure…why? Oh…you're thinking about those missing women."

"Yeah, do you remember seeing him with either Martha Rowley or Kathy Stanwick?"

"No. Besides, Mr. Grant is really nice. Just last night, he walked a college student home after her roommate ditched her here."

"Thanks Brenda. I've really got to run. I'll be back."

"Good to see you back."

Meg walked out of Joe's and looked back down the street where Trevor had disappeared. She walked back to her car and got in. Meg drove to the station to see if there were any outstanding warrants on Trevor Grant.

CHAPTER 28

The two days flew by, and Meg was no closer to finding a suspect. The search continued for Kathy, but mostly people from the gospel church that were friends of the Stanwicks. She even saw Jake in the woods searching with George. Meg was afraid to approach George and be reprimanded again, so she went back to the paper work instead of searching through the woods. She remembered Jake's frustration four years ago looking for some clue that would tie all the cases together and to one person. It was a fluke that those clothes were found in the hotel room that Angelos had been living in.

Meg drove down the Northway toward Albany, knowing she would be late for her Thursday morning meeting with Reggie. She was annoyed when Pete called her saying he was going to be in the meeting with her and could he go over evidence before they met with the captain. That meant one thing to Meg, Reggie didn't trust her and was giving the case to Pete.

But when Dr. Chevers had agreed to meet with her this morning before his first class at the college, Meg knew it could save her case. If he gave her the missing piece of information, it wouldn't matter to Reggie that she was late. Somehow, that old man was tied to this case and Dr. Chevers had the answer to how.

Meg pulled into the parking lot at the college. She wasn't familiar with the campus but it was small and it should be easy to find the literature department. Meg caught her reflection in the mirror and grimaced. She didn't have time to take a shower this morning and she was wearing the clothes she wore over the weekend. She ran her fingers through her hair and then shrugged. Meg finally found Dr. Chevers twenty minutes later in the cafeteria having a cup of coffee.

"Dr. Chevers," Meg said showing her badge. "I'm Det. Riley. We've been emailing…."

"Yes, detective. Please, have a cup of coffee."

Meg sat down at that table and took a cup of black coffee. He waited for her to begin. "As you know, I've been working on a case up near Saratoga. There have been these strange animal hairs that seem to match hairs from a few cases in London."

"I did get your email. I know what you are talking about."

"What I don't understand is the species the hairs came from. The information from Interpol was not clear and then one of the clerks emailed me one of your articles."

"Well, the police are skeptical of anything that isn't the norm. Of course, you are an exception."

"I just want to have all the information."

"Certainly. Well, legend tells of a wolf like creature that is part wolf and part werewolf. The Irish folklore tale that began during the 1800s spoke of a man that caught a werewolf. Curious, he decided to mate it with a wolf. It produced another creature. One that was wild, yet understands what people say. The man decided to keep them as pets. But since they are wild at heart, they cannot be fully tamed. And he found they didn't die," he ended with flair and waiting for Meg's reaction.

"So, people believe the same animals are living today?"

"Precisely. The man had to tell his son as he aged. His son became the new keeper of the creatures and made sure they continued to live. It was passed down through the generations."

"They?"

"Yes, a male and a female."

"What is the name of this family?"

"The original clan was the O'Shanauty. But they died out and a boy was picked from a neighboring clan. Those clan names have been lost over time."

"Does the name Shamus O'Leary mean anything to you?"

"No, but it is Irish. Doesn't mean anything though."

"If this was a clan secret, how did you find this story?"

"They are wild beasts. People have seen them over the years. They have, at times, been taken over by their nature and attacked villages."

"We have women that are just missing. No evidence that they've been attacked by animals."

"Then it would be the keeper. He must be getting old and needs a new one."

"Why would he be taking women?"

"There is a ritual of blood that passes the care of the creatures to a new person. It requires four women, a full moon, and the creatures acceptance of the new keeper chosen."

"So if my animal hairs are from these 'creatures,' four women will disappear?"

"Yes. And then they will be sacrificed."

"Dr. Chevers, how do I find this person?"

"In the early days, they were hunted. Now, you must find the creatures. They will lead you to the keeper."

"But how?"

"Detective, if it was simple, it would have already been done. But I must caution you, this is folklore, a myth to most. No one will believe you. I believe these creatures exist. But I'm a crazy professor that is allowed to weave tales."

"What am I going to do then?"

"Find the keeper. They can't exist without him."

CHAPTER 29

Pete sat at his desk in the squad room. Reggie called him in for a meeting with Meg and he wasn't too happy about it. He glanced up at the clock and then at his watch. Meg was late and it was making Pete nervous. Finally, Pete got up and went to Reggie's office. He knocked on the door and waited. Reggie called out for him to come in.

Reggie had his back to the door. As Pete walked through the door, Reggie said, "A little late you two. You know how I feel about punctuality."

"Uh, it's just me."

Reggie swung the chair around. "Where's Riley?"

"I don't know. She was supposed to be here to go over a few things before we met with you."

"I don't like this Burgess. She's become this loose cannon that I can't control. She better get here with a reasonable explanation or she'll be facing disciplinary actions. She's been late for meetings, talking crazy."

Pete put his hands up in surrender. "I agree with you boss. I think her theories are a little off, but I know she's doing a good job investigating."

Reggie leaned back in his chair and it screeched in protest. "You coming around to her way of thinking?"

"No, not at all. There's a person out there. Two women are already missing and then the Craig woman dies. I think they are all connected."

"Well, it just got worse." Reggie opened a folder on the pile of paperwork on his desk, pulled out a picture, and handed it to Pete. "This is a high school graduation picture of Lauren Thomas. Her roommate, a Liz Salisbury, reported her missing. She's a student at the community college and she was out a few nights ago. Salisbury said she thinks some foreign guy picked her up and they went somewhere."

"Could she be with the guy who picked her up?"

"That's a possibility, but according to the roommate, Lauren was a good student. Never missed a class. She's been missing for a few days already. Go check it out. This is the report that she filed. Go to the campus and talk to this Salisbury girl. Find this foreign dude and hopefully we find the missing student. Find her before the evening news."

The door swung opened and Meg rushed in. She was disheveled. Her hair was half falling out of its ponytail that Meg had thrown in earlier in the day. Her blouse that had a coffee stain on it was partially untucked from her wrinkled pants. She was carrying a fat expanding folder with papers half falling out of it. As she sat down next to Pete, he could smell her body odor. He leaned away from her to avoid the smell. She was a mess.

"Sorry I'm late. I was down in Albany talking to someone from the historical society."

"And that's was worth being late for yet another meeting Riley?" Reggie's voice was low and dangerous.

Meg nervously wet her lips. "I was following a lead and the time got away from me."

"And?"

"I know you don't like my theory, so…um…I'll just…"

"Just what? Waste more time? Did it even occur to you that these women may be alive somewhere? Did it occur to you that leaving us out of your investigation harms the ability of this force to aid in solving this case?"

"I'm a good investigator. I think I've proved myself over the years. I've been following a theory that I realize no one wants to accept, but there are people who actually believe that I may be right."

"Right? Right about what? What have you shown ME that could persuade ME, YOUR boss that you are right?" Reggie jumped to his feet and slammed his fist on the desk. "You talk about animal hairs, beasts that howl at the moon, and I'm stuck in this office scrambling to get other cops to do your investigative work. Tell me what you have, in hard evidence about a person, so that I can continue to support your ability to handle this investigation."

Meg sat stunned and looked at Pete for support. But Pete was staring at a chip in the corner of Reggie's desk and wouldn't look at her. Meg looked down at her file on her lap and began to pull papers out.

"There is this guy at the historical society teaching a class at a college in Albany…."

"This guy? Who is this guy? Does he have a name, credentials?"

"Harry Chevers. He has a PhD in medieval folklore…"

"Medieval folklore? Are you seriously sitting in my office talking about this Chevers, Mr. PhD in medieval folklore in the same breath and context as missing women from Granelle?"

"It's the hairs. There were hairs found like these in London. They are so unusual because they aren't normal wolf hairs. Dr. Chevers explained that there were some werewolves that were bred with wolves. These hairs are believed to come from their offspring. Part werewolf, part wolf."

Meg looked over at Pete who was staring at her like she had lost her mind. She glanced up at Reggie and saw a mixture of the same disbelief and pure anger. She fumbled in the papers she had and pulled out some that had been printed from the Internet.

When neither man said anything, she went on. "According to London, these mutant werewolves never travel alone but are protected by a person or a keeper. Someone that helps them survive."

Reggie sat down hard in his chair. The springs groaned against his weight. He lost the angry look and looked really concerned at Meg. He turned to Pete and said, "Get out of here and follow up on that other case we were talking about. Get Matthews to work it with you. I need to talk to Riley."

Pete got up and left feeling relieved to be getting out of the office. Reggie turned his attention to Meg.

"What's going on with you, Riley?"

""I'm investigating all the angles here, Captain. I know how it sounds…."

"Don't presume you know how it sounds to me," Reggie shouted.

Meg cringed knowing it would be heard in the squad room. But she didn't back down. "Captain…"

"And don't interrupt me. Facts, that's what I'm interested in. Two women are missing, presumed dead. I want that creep found. Not some story about mutant werewolves. And look at you. You're a mess. When's the last time you looked in a mirror, Riley? I think you're losing it. Maybe you need to take some of your vacation time."

"Will you listen to me for a minute," Meg fought her desire to yell at him. "Have you looked at the forensic evidence I have? No, you haven't. You want facts. I have facts. Will you listen? No. You have it set in your mind that you're going to find another Angelos out there. I'm convinced that there is a regular person involved. Dr. Chevers talked about someone called the keeper. I haven't found him yet, but I have a lead on someone. As far as my personal hygiene comes into play in this, it's just that, personal."

Reggie leaned forward in the chair causing the springs to groan again. "You listen to me. I am in charge here, not you. I want you to take a few days off."

"I don't need time off. What I need is support from my boss. I know this sounds bizarre and I am pursuing other leads. But there is evidence to support this theory. Will you please look at the evidence?"

Reggie pulled a file from the corner of his desk and began thumbing through it. He didn't look back at Meg. "Take a few days off. You will report to me Monday at 9:00 am. Don't be late."

Meg pulled the papers out of the file. She went through them and took out three sheets. She stood up and put the rest of the file on the chair Pete had just left and pushed the papers in front of Reggie.

"This report is from the Angelos file. It clearly shows the DNA from animal hairs that were found on the clothes of one of the victims. This one is from hairs found in the front seat of the Stanwick's car. This report was just faxed over to me from Scotland Yards. Look at the reports, chief." She pointed to each page and talked fast in case Reggie told her to get out. "The DNA is identical. It's not just similar, it's identical. Jake said we live in upstate New York and it's not uncommon to find animal hairs at crime scenes. I'm not talking about finding a dog hair of a similar type. This animal, this particular animal, was at different crime scenes here and around England. How does an animal get from England to Granelle? That's where a person comes into play. I want to find that person."

She stood waiting while Reggie read the pages. He looked up at her and shook his head. "Riley, animals don't open doors, stab people, or shoot them. Stanwick was in her car."

"We don't know whether Stanwick opened her own car door and then was attacked, and I already said that there is a person involved. Look if you don't like the angle; let me work it on my own. If you want to tell people that Pete is working the case and I'm on vacation, that's fine. But I need to have your support as my boss. I'm a good detective. You see that there is some evidence to substantiate my theory. Can you please support me?"

Reggie rifled through the papers once more and shook his head. "Can't do it, Riley."

"Well, that's just fine then. I'll take my vacation, but you can't tell me what to do with my personal time." Meg snatched the papers out of Reggie's hands and put them on the top of the pile of papers, startling Reggie.

"Riley!" he shouted. "You listen to me, I'm going to make myself very clear here. You are out of control and I will not allow you to tamper with this case anymore. If I find you anywhere near these cases, you'll be fired."

"That's totally unfair. I have evidence...."

"You better get out of here, Riley. Take your vacation. Now!"

Riley stood staring back at him. Finally, she turned, picked up her pile of papers and left the office. Meg stormed out of the station and to her car.

As she drove back to the motel, she kept replaying the past few days in her head. A week ago she had a life that included a fiancé, a place to live, and a job. Meg was trying hard to believe that she needed the vacation, but she couldn't. She knew that the theory that she got from Dr. Chevers was right and that the animal was in Granelle, somewhere. She had to find the keeper and somehow she knew it was O'Leary.

Back at the hotel, Meg found her makeup bag buried in a box in her trunk and her hair dryer. She went into her room, took a hot shower, and took her time putting on her makeup. An hour later, Meg was changed into a white silk blouse and her hunter green blazer. Looking at herself in the mirror, Meg felt more like herself and more in control again. She called Maureen and told her she would take the house. She made plans to meet her at the house to sign the lease and get the keys.

CHAPTER 30

Trevor walked into the house. He had been out all night and most of the day. He didn't want to leave Kathy, but he finally relented to Shamus's demands. It bothered Trevor because he only needed one more and this set back his plan. With the female wolf sick, Trevor knew he needed to act quickly to complete the circle ritual and make the boy part of their family. He left Kathy in the cave he found deep in the woods. He had wanted to kill her first, but that was another fight he lost with Shamus. Lately, Trevor felt Shamus was displeased with everything he did.

The dense bushes in the woods had left scratches on his arms and face. Trevor walked down the basement stairs. Shamus was in the common room packing a crate and looked up as Trevor walked up to him. Shamus hesitated only a moment before going back to his packing.

"Don't try to stop me. I've told you that we should have left last week. Things are getting dangerous. But since you won't leave with me, I've decided to leave anyway. I want to see my great granddaughter before I die," Shamus said.

Trevor put his hand on Shamus's arm stopping him from packing. The two men looked at each other. Trevor saw for the first time that his long time friend was an old man. "You know you can't leave. What about her?"

Trevor looked over at where the pallet had been. The area was clean and everything was put away. Shamus answered before Trevor could ask. "She's gone. I thought she was recovering, but she died."

"But she can't die."

"And why not?"

"They are immortal."

"Are they? Nay, Trevor that is the myth. The reality is, they can die."

"They have lived so long, recovering from wounds before."

Shamus turned and faced Trevor. "Don't believe the myths, they are just that. They are but flesh and blood. They die."

"I won't believe this."

"Believe what you want. It doesn't matter anymore."

"What about me? I'm flesh and blood. Look at me." Trevor spread his arms out. "Are you going to say that I'm going to die too?"

"You don't see what I see. I've seen the darkness that we live in, but I've also seen a light that you can't see. Besides, these old myths are just falsehoods. If these creatures were immortal, the earth would be filled with werewolves, vampires, and other demonic creatures. But it is not."

"This is ridiculous and we are wasting time. Come let's find her."

"You can't. I buried her in the woods. I'm going back to Ireland. I have my ticket waiting. I already called Kelly and told her I'm coming home."

"Kelly? The daughter who scorned you."

"Aye, she scorned the life I led. I neglected her and my family to follow the creatures. But I'm too old to lead this life anymore."

"That's just it Shamus, we almost have the boy...."

"With the boy, you don't need me. He will be trained to take my place. But you are running out of time. Things have been set into place that you can no longer control. He will be back and when he realizes she is gone, you won't be able to control him. I don't want to be here to face his wrath. You should leave with me."

Trevor regarded his friend for a moment. "Go Shamus. Things won't be the way you suggest, but go. I can't stop you."

Trevor turned to leave and Shamus reached out and grabbed his arm. "You've been like my son all these years and we have traveled for a long time together. Please be careful. You will find that I am right. When he comes back...and it's not just him you need to be worried about. There is a preacher whose been praying. I've seen him questioning things. He is dangerous to you if he decides to come after you. You may need to leave here soon before you are discovered. It will be as the old days and they will hunt you."

"Shamus, you are talking foolishness. We have skirted the law before and as for a preacher...he can't have me burned at the stake." Trevor laughed. "This isn't the old days. People don't believe in us anymore. As you said, we are a myth. My only regret is that you are leaving. But this is your choice."

"Aye, but you can still come with me. Leave here."

For a long moment, they both looked at each other. Trevor shook his head and walked into a back room. Shamus finished his packing and took the crate upstairs. In the kitchen, he looked around before going out the door. He set the crate down next to the car and opened the trunk. He picked the crate up and tucked it in the trunk next to an old battered suitcase.

Shamus got into the car and started it. As he put the car in reverse to back out of the driveway, he looked up and saw the creature standing in front of the car and slowly let up on the gas. As the car crept backwards, the creature walked toward the car. Shamus looked behind him to see if there were any cars coming just as the creature jumped on the hood of the car. Shamus backed the car out onto the road and then looked up at the creature on the hood of the car. Their eyes locked and the creature snarled.

Shamus stomped at the gas and the creature slid off the hood scratching the heavy metal. Shamus put the car into drive and stepped on the gas again. Looking in the rearview mirror, he saw the creature standing in the road watching him drive away. As the car disappeared around a corner, the creature headed back into the woods.

CHAPTER 31

Sam sat on the picnic table in the backyard. The yard was full of dead leaves and it was cold outside. Karen had already packed up and moved downstate with their aunt. The house was on the market and Sam hated seeing the sign on the front lawn. They were supposed to stay until the house was sold, but his father had decided to leave this weekend for Poughkeepsie. Stanley had already resigned from his job and his brother-in-law had found him another accounting position downstate. Once they moved, his aunt would be staying with Sam after school so that he wouldn't be alone anymore.

Sam was supposed to be going through the boxes in the attic. Instead, he sat in the backyard, thinking about losing his mother, his friends, and his house all in the same month. He hated his life. Just when Melinda was getting friendly with him again, he was going to move.

"Hey, Sam."

The voice startled Sam and he turned. Trevor stood smiling at him. "Oh, hi. I didn't hear you coming."

"You looked pretty lost in thought. I saw the sign. Moving?"

"Yeah, Dad wants to move down near his sister for now."

"He told me that last week when your sister left. How's the house sale going?"

"I don't know. It doesn't matter anyway. We're leaving in a few days."

"Oh, I thought you would be staying until the house sold."

"We were, but Uncle Kyle found my Dad a job already. He has to start it next week."

"That's too bad. Just when we were becoming friends."

Sam shrugged not knowing what to say. Trevor stood thinking for a few minutes. The timing wasn't right, but he didn't want to lose Sam now.

"I've got to get back to packing," Sam said as he stood to go back in the house.

"Wait a minute. I actually came by for another reason. I was exploring in the woods behind our houses when I found some caves. I think I found some of your stuff in it."

"Probably, I go out there sometimes."

"Is that where you were when you ran away?"

Sam spun around. "I got lost," he said in a quiet voice.

"Others might not see it that way when they realize that the stuff is yours."

"Are you going to tell my Dad?"

Trevor laughed softly. "No, of course not. But you may want to get your stuff out of the woods before someone else finds them. I hear there is another girl missing and they may send searchers out again. It wouldn't be good if someone else found your stuff and came to the same conclusions I did. Someone may even think you had something to do with your mother's unfortunate accident."

Sam looked scared. "You think someone might think that?"

"Adults are like that. They may even think you're bad enough to go to a reform school instead of being able to start over again in a new town."

"Man. I told everyone I was lost. They would know I lied."

"Exactly. Why don't we go get your stuff?"

"You'll help me?"

"Sure, let's go before your father decides to come look for you."

"Okay." Sam headed toward the woods and Trevor smiled as he followed him.

When they reached the caves, Trevor stopped Sam. "Come with me first. I want to show you something in another cave."

The smell from the cave was foul and Sam tried to breathe through his mouth so that he couldn't smell it. Before his eyes could adjust to the darkness of the cave, he could see the glowing eyes in the interior of the cave. Sam turned to run out and was caught by Trevor.

"It's alright, Sam. He wants to meet you," Trevor said softly.

Sam shook his head and tried to push away from Trevor, but Trevor was too strong for him. Sam felt the hot breath of the creature behind him and froze against Trevor, too frightened to fight.

"That's better, my friend. Do you remember when we met I told you that if you were my friend, he would never hurt you? Well, now he wants you to be his friend also."

Trevor turned Sam around. Sam had his eyes shut tight afraid to look at the creature. Trevor continued in a soothing voice. "You see it was time for us to have another. Shamus, my other friend, was old and was unable to continue. You have proven to me that you are a child worthy to join us. The loss of your mother gives you the freedom to become my child. The way has been prepared for you. We just need to do the sacrifices. And you just need to do your part in order to become one with us."

Trevor moved Sam toward the back of the cave. Sam opened his eyes to find himself being pushed into a cage. He turned to run as Trevor closed the door. Trevor put a large padlock on the door and turned away. Sam grabbed the bars of the cage and watched as Trevor lit a match. He lit a lantern that was on the cave's ledge.

As light filled the cave, Sam saw clearly the creature sitting in the middle of the cave. It looked like a large wolf and its eyes had a red glow even in the light from the lantern. In his wildest imagination, Sam could never fathom the terror he felt being locked in a cage with the wolf sitting there watching him. As Sam watched, the wolf got up and walked to the cage. Sam's terror mounted and to his relief, he fainted.

CHAPTER 32

Jake forced himself to look at the stack of church bills that Mrs. Baxter had left on Pastor Walt's desk for Jake to approve. He knew he had to get through the stack since Mr. Richman would be coming by the church in the morning to sign the checks. But Jake's mind wasn't on the bills or on the long list Mrs. Baxter had left him to do. Jake heard the office door open and moaned.

Jake looked up expecting to see one of the church members, but was surprised to see Reggie.

"Hey Reggie, what brings you to the church?" Jake said standing.

Reggie waved him to sit as he said, "You got a few minutes for an old friend?" Reggie didn't wait for a reply, just went on as he sat down. "Hear about Riley's theory on the Stanwick case?"

Jake realized he was still holding the telephone bill and set it on the pile. "Yeah, I heard some. What do you think?"

Reggie leaned back in his chair and shook his head. "I don't believe in fairy tales, monsters, or feral beasts eating our citizens. I don't care about unknown animal hairs. I care about a crazy person out there in our little town and missing women. Someone like Angelos. Do you follow me?"

"I think so. You think the cases are tied together?"

"Not the way Riley does. It could be a copycat, but maybe not. I know that it's similar, but not exactly either. What does bother me, though, is a call I got from Coxsackie. I didn't need to hear that Angelos is having some kind of a breakdown. If the press gets a hold of it and Riley shoots her mouth off, this office will be up to its ears in a PR problem."

"Why are you here?"

"Actually, it's about the calls from Coxsackie."

"What's up?"

"Angelos went psycho or something last night. He attacked two other inmates and tried biting them like he was a dog or something. They put him in solitary and he's been asking to see you."

"Why would he want to see me?"

"Don't know. But he's been sedated. The warden called me to see if you can come out and to see if it will calm Angelos down or something."

Jake just stared at Reggie, who was waiting for a response. Finally Jake said, "I don't know what to tell you, Reggie. I can't go down to Coxsackie right now. I've got an elder's prayer breakfast in the morning, a couple of other appointments and I really need to run down to Albany to visit the Ryersons."

"Jake, I need you to come back and help out the force."

Jake shook his head. "I can't do that. Look at this desk. I've got my own problems to deal with. Most of which I don't know how to handle."

Reggie sat forward in his chair. "Look, I'm not asking you to give all this up. But this is a major problem for us. We've lost three people on the force in the last two months. I had to put Riley on leave. Pete doesn't have the experience to run an investigation on his own. I've got Greg Matthews doing routine police calls. Trudy Parker is on dispatch and old Marty Driscole trying to do all the lab work. That leaves me, alone. If you can at least go to Coxsackie and find out what's going on."

Jake was already shaking his head. "I've got so many of my own problems. Ron Richman is coming in the morning to sign these checks. I've got about five people with problems that I'm trying to work with. Then, there are the Craigs and Stanwicks. I've got nothing for the Sunday sermon. If Pastor Walt wasn't in the hospital, it would be different. But I made a commitment to this church. I'm sorry, but I just can't."

"Jake, you said you wanted to help the people of Granelle. Don't you think that God can use you as a cop as much as a preacher?"

"Of course, He can. But I can't just walk away. The church is in just as big crisis as the force."

"How can you say that, three women are missing," Reggie said getting louder.

"I can say that because one of the missing women is a member of my church. Her husband is a friend of mine and is struggling. So my training in law enforcement is helping me help him as his minister. I'm able to help him because I understand how investigations work, not to mention what the Craigs are going through. I was able to help Mrs. Buchanan when she was arrested. I can see how God is using my training to help people through hard situations in life."

"But what about the criminal out there that has these women?"

"I don't know, just like I don't know about all this paperwork or about the politics in a church. But I believe that I'm where God wants me to be right now and I'll be praying for you Reggie."

Reggie shook his head. "I need more help than that."

Just then the phone rang. As Jake answered it, Reggie got up to leave. Jake gestured for him to wait and then hung up.

"Looks like we got another joint problem. That was Stanley Craig. His son is missing again." Jake sighed as he looked at the pile on his desk. "I better leave a note for Mr. Richman. Hope he understands."

CHAPTER 33

Jake sat in the Craigs' living room watching the activity all around him. Reggie had organized another search and was directing searchers into the woods. Even though Sam had only been gone a few hours, Reggie had already called the state police back to help again. The searchers looked tired from the long days of searching for the missing women.

When Jake told Mrs. Baxter, she sent the women's auxiliary over with dinner. The women were in the kitchen organizing dinner for the searchers and looking for other chores to do. Mrs. Baxter had also called Coach Morgan who already had his team in the woods again.

"Okay," Reggie said sitting down next to Jake. "I don't think we're going to find the kid in the woods. I need someone to go door to door. I want you to do that."

"Won't that compromise your investigation if I come up with a lead?"

"No. I want you to call me if you find anything suspicious and I'll be right there. I need to stay here. You're qualified to do this."

"I know. Where do you want me to start?"

"There's an old house at the end of the road. Try there first, and then work your way back up the road. If the missing women were being kept anywhere in the woods, we would have found them by now. Take one of the men from your church with you."

"I'll take Dave Jacobs."

"Is he already in the woods?" Reggie asked looking outside.

"Not likely. If anything, he's probably at the church calling people to pray for the Craigs."

Someone called out Reggie's name. As he started walking away, he said, "Get moving, and keep me informed."

Jake didn't have to wait long for Dave to show up. Getting in his car with him, Jake directed him down to the dead end. He explained they were going to ask neighbors if they saw Sam. As they pulled up in front of the old Hanson house, Jake looked around. There was no car in the driveway and the house looked abandoned. They got out of the car and walked to the porch.

"Are you sure that Mr. Bennett said to start here?" Dave asked. "Far as I know, this place has been empty for a long time."

"That may make this place perfect for committing a crime. A vagrant could easily move in and no one would know."

Jake noticed that the porch was dusty and covered with cobwebs. He peered through a dirty window and saw covered furniture. Dave knocked on the door and it echoed into the house. They waited a few minutes and Dave knocked again. No one came to the door. Jake walked off the porch and walked to the side of the house.

"Pastor Jake?" Dave called out. "Where are you going? Is that considered trespassing?"

"Not when we have missing people in town," he replied as he walked around the house. Jake noticed the signs that someone had been living there. He saw the fire pit where someone had burned trash. The back porch looked like it was the door that was used and the yard was trampled. But otherwise, it didn't look like anyone was there. Jake still went to the back door and knocked.

"Hello," Jake called out peaking into a window. He saw a kitchen that looked clean. He was sure that someone was living there. After a few more attempts to get someone to answer, Jake walked off the porch and found Dave nervously waiting by the car.

"Well, someone is living here. Whoever it is uses the back as an entrance," Jake said. "Come on, let's go visit some of the other neighbors."

Dave looked relieved as he got back in the car. He didn't like walking into people's backyards and certainly didn't like something about this house.

Down in the basement, Trevor sat quietly. He stroked the head of the wolf that lay near him growling. Trevor had just made it back to the house and had locked Sam in the basement. Without Shamus to help him, he was nervous and beginning to feel like his plans were going to fail. This was too close and he recognized that voice that had called out. That cop got too close before and they had to run. Maybe he needed to change his plans. That cop turned preacher needed some more problems to keep him off his scent. The full moon was coming soon, and Trevor needed to be ready.

As he listened to the sound of the car driving off, Trevor pulled out his cell phone. He knew what to do this time. He'd get the preacher too. He knew Shamus wouldn't approve, but Shamus couldn't stop him now. He listened as Meg's voice told him to leave a message. He left a message asking her to meet him for dinner and to call back soon.

CHAPTER 34

Jake looked through the glass window in his door and was surprised to see Meg standing on the porch. He closed his eyes and prayed for wisdom. Meg knocked again.

"Jake, I know you're there. Please let me in," Meg said softly. Jake sighed and looked at Buddy. He shook his head. Buddy whined and wagged his tail.

He opened the door, but blocked the opening with his body. "What's up, Meg?" he said casually.

Meg took a deep breath. "Can I come in? I need to talk to you about what's been going on in Granelle."

"Meg, I know that you've been removed from the case and you're supposed to be on 'vacation.'"

"Jake, you have to talk to me. He's after me now. I'm afraid." Meg looked around her as if someone could be listening to her. "Plus, it's cold out here. Please, if you ever loved me…"

"Don't go there Meg."

"Please let me come in just to get warm then."

"Okay, okay. But I'm not going to talk to you about the case," Jake moved and opened the door up. He gestured toward the living room. Buddy saw Meg and ran up to her, jumping and wagging his tail.

"Hi, Buddy. How you been, boy?" Meg said letting the big dog jump on her and petting him.

"Okay, Buddy. Go lay down," Jake said, pushing the dog down and pointing toward the kitchen. Buddy got down and walked toward the kitchen. Jake took Meg's arm and led her to the couch. Jake sat in the chair across from her and waited.

Meg looked around nervously. "I know you don't want to talk to me about the cases. But I'm scared."

"It's not that I don't want to talk to you about the cases. I'm trying hard not to be involved. I have my own work now. There is a lot of administrative work that I didn't even know about."

Meg nodded and looked down at her hands. "I understand. But I'm afraid that I'm going to be the next one to disappear."

"Why would you think that?"

"Remember I told you I found those hairs?" Jake nodded. "I was working on a theory about these animal hairs and found information about a kind of werewolf like creature. I even talked to a doctor who is supposedly an authority on folklore and he weeds out the fantasy from the fact. He said that these creatures are real. But Bennett…"

"I know, I talked to Reggie. He doesn't believe it."

"At the time, I had doubts myself. But I had the forensic evidence that showed that it was the same animal hair that was here and in England. Then…well, I saw the animal I'm afraid. It's huge and it's threatening and it's…"

"What do you want from me?"

"I want you to believe me," she said passionately. Jake stared into her green eyes. He knew she believed it, but he couldn't.

"I believe that you believe it."

"No, believe it. It's true."

"Meg," Jake started and looked down, away from those eyes. She got off the couch and knelt by the chair he was sitting in. She reach out and grabbed his arm.

"Don't Jake. Look at me. You know me better than anyone else. I'm not lying to you. I saw it myself. It looks like a big wolf…."

"You can lose your job over this. All I have to do is call Bennett."

"Is that what you really want to do? Report me? Besides, I don't care about losing my job. I'm talking about some kind of unbelievable horror. It knows where I'm living. The guy with it knows my number…."

"Guy?"

Meg dropped her hands. "Yeah, it's this guy. He has my cell phone number."

"What do you want from me?" Jake asked again.

"I want you to help me kill it."

Jake stared at her in disbelief. "Kill…?"

"The creature."

"Meg," he said softly.

"Don't patronize me. I came here to ask you for help. I'm not out there in the woods hunting that thing alone. I don't know of any other person that I could trust with this. That's why I'm here."

"Trust? I can't do this. Even if I believed there was some animal in the woods, we just can't go into the woods with guns drawn. And what about the missing people? This is a police matter. You're risking your career in pursuit of some animal that you believe is out there somewhere."

"I saw that creature outside my house last night. It tracked me down. Trevor keeps calling me on my cell phone trying to get me out at night. I think he is the lure to get the girls out in the open for the creature to kill. I've never known such terror as I felt last night. I looked out the window and it was staring right into my eyes. Then the phone would ring." She shuddered. "Brenda, the bartender at Joe's, mentioned that Trevor seems to hit on single women. I know that you probably hate me for what happened between us, but I don't know where else to turn. I'm afraid to go home tonight. What if Trevor comes?"

"Hold on. Hold on. The bartender told you that this guy hits on single women?"

Meg nodded. "She knows Trevor is interested in me. He comes in, picks up girls who are alone and look lonely."

"Kathy Stanwick is married. And was far as I know, she wasn't a person to go out to bars at night."

"So what are you saying?"

"Your theory is flawed."

"You know it all…right?" Meg started getting riled up.

"No, I know the Stanwicks. She doesn't fit the profile of women that you just described. And don't you think that maybe your judgment is clouded if you think some man that asked you out is a killer? You're not being impartial."

"Well, now we get the great detective Jake's theory," she said coolly.

"I'm just trying to stop you from destroying your career and look at this from a different perspective. In the Angelos case, all the women were single and young. But what about Kathy. She doesn't fit the profile, and for that matter, you don't either."

"What's that suppose to mean?"

"You're engaged, certainly not considered single and available."

"Oh…that…I'm not engaged anymore," she said looking at her hand. She held it up. "See no ring anymore."

"I'm sorry, Meg," Jake said sincerely. She looked to see if he was being sarcastic, and finding nothing in his look, she nodded.

"Yeah, tough break."

"Where are you staying now?"

"I rented a house on Consul Road."

"Can you see that with all that's been going on personally with you that you might be wrong in thinking that this man is after you?"

"I don't know about that Jake."

"I do and you need to step back and really look at your evidence. You're a good cop, Meg, but you're a little bit off here. I don't want to see you going out on a hunt for some animal in the woods."

"I guess you're right. Maybe I'll just go home and get some rest. Sure you don't want to come back to the force?"

Jake smiled. "I've thought about it with all the problems that I've had to deal with this past month. But Pastor Walt is recovering and should be back soon. I get to be second banana again. I can't wait."

"Well, guess I better get going," Meg said standing. Jake looked at her as she reached down to pet Buddy.

"Meg," Jake said a little hesitantly. "Something's still not right."

"What makes you say that?" she said not looking at him.

"I know you and you kind of gave up too quick. It's almost like you're just trying to pacify me. You aren't going after that animal are you?"

"Look, I'll admit I was obsessed with finding the creature. I thought about the folklore and proving it to be true. But no one will believe me unless I show them the carcass of the animal."

"So you still plan to go after it?"

"Yes, and then shoot them both with silver bullets."

"Both? Are there two of them?"

"A male and a female. You thought so, too. Remember the night at the Stanwicks?"

"I told you it was a dog."

"I've got to get the creatures. Maybe Trevor will just go away once they are dead."

"How are they all tied to this guy?"

"I'm not sure they are. But we…I need to investigate the possibility."

"Okay, but what are you going to do now?"

"Go pay him a visit."

"Are you crazy?"

"Hey, I have a legitimate police matter to discuss with the man and hopefully will be able to find out something about the wolf at the same time."

"Meg you can't do this. Don't get in the middle of this case."

"There's one other thing," Meg hesitated. "Dr. Chevers told me that there is a ritual that is performed. It's to make a new keeper. It was tied to some folklore in Ireland. I have to get this resolved before the full moon."

"What you are telling me is just the stuff of myth. There is very little truth in this."

Meg shook her head, "You can't know that."

"Meg, look you want me to believe in werewolves and folklore stuff. But I know that what I believe is true. It changed my life, not just the stuff between us, but…"

"Now you're going to go off on that religion kick." Meg was staring at the floor with a disgusted look on her face.

"You know I'm a Christian." Jake stood and lifted her chin so she was looking at him. "Meg, I know that the power of God is stronger than anything that is evil. I have Jesus in my life and nothing Satanic, cults, werewolves, whatever, can harm me. You said that you were afraid. There is a verse in the Bible that says, 'my God is a warrior, when I stand in His strength I will not be afraid.' (NIV) Will you let me pray for you?"

"No, I don't want any of that religious stuff."

"But you're willing to risk your life for something that is folklore?"

"It's real!"

"Is it? Have you considered the possibility that this man may have trained a dog and that he is crazy? Maybe he finds the same stuff on the internet that you did and decides to make it real. Does that make it real? No, it just means this man is another psychopath that the police need to find before anyone else gets killed."

Jake looked at her for a long moment and the phone rang. Jake picked up a cordless phone and took it into the other room. Meg shook her head and sat on the couch. Buddy came over and laid his head on her lap. Absent mindedly, she began petting his head. She could hear Jake's voice in the other room, but couldn't make out what he was saying. Jake walked back into the room and stood in the doorway watching Meg pet Buddy. Meg looked up expectantly.

"I've got to go out for a while. That kid ran away again and his father is having a bad time. It's been so rough on the family since Mrs. Craig died, and they are members of my church," Jake went to the closet and pulled out his jacket. Meg stood to leave. "You can stay here if you want. Buddy can keep you company."

"It's okay. I'd better just go."

Meg stood and walked over to the door. "Are you sure you're going to be okay? You can stay until I get back and we can talk more."

"I'll be fine. I think I'll go down to Albany and see my parents."

Meg walked past him and outside. She pulled her jacket around her as she stepped off the porch. Buddy tried to follow her, but Jake stopped him.

"Sorry, Buddy," he said patting him on the head. "You've got to stay. I'll be back soon...I hope." As Jake locked the door and pulled it closed behind him, Buddy whined and pawed at the door. He lifted his head and sniffed at the air. Whining again, he turned and ran up the stairs and under Jake's bed.

CHAPTER 35

Jake took the now familiar route to the Craig's house feeling somewhat depressed. He knew Stanley was having a difficult time dealing with the loss of his wife and that Sam was blaming himself. Now with Meg talking about going off on a wild goose chase, he felt helpless. As he thought of all the things he felt responsible for, Jake began to pray.

As Jake pulled into the Craig's driveway, a gust of wind blew dry leaves across the lawn. Jake saw the For Sale sign blow in the wind and thought of Sam and Kathy being out in the cold night somewhere. As he opened the car door and looked at the cars in the driveway, he knew that searchers were still out in the woods looking for the missing.

Coach Morgan came out of the front door as Jake walked up. The men shook hands. "He's not doing so good, Pastor Jake."

"It's been a tough time for the family."

"Sure has been. You think the kid ran away?"

"I don't know what to think. I just keep praying that he is found safe and sound, regardless of the circumstances. Stanley can't handle too much more."

"Well, I was just going to get on home. I've got to get up early for football practice in the morning."

"Okay…thanks for the call."

Jake walked into the house and paused at the door. He felt like he was being watched. He turned and watched the coach pull his pickup out of the driveway and he waved. He didn't see the dark shape watching him from across the street. As the door closed behind Jake, the dark shadow ran off into the woods.

* * *

Meg sat in her car in front of her rented house looking around. Finally, she opened the door quickly and ran to the front door. She slammed the door and locked it behind her. She went into the kitchen and dropped her purse on the cluttered kitchen table. She looked at her file on the cases and picked it up. Meg held the file for a minute and then shook her head. She put the file into an empty box that was on the floor. Moving some junk on the table to one side, she reached across the table for her laptop, but the cord lay on the table. The spot that her laptop was sitting was empty.

Meg reached into her purse and pulled out a small gun. She checked the kitchen door and found it locked. She quickly looked around the kitchen and her cell phone rang. Startled she pulled it out of her pocket. "Hello," she said answering the phone.

"Finally came home?" the voice said.

"Who is this?"

"Trevor," he said surprised. "Were you expecting someone else?"

"No. I wasn't expecting you either."

"Well, I wanted to know if you would like to go out for dinner tonight."

"I'm tired. I didn't have a good night last night."

"I'm sorry to hear that."

"Are you?"

"Of course. I'd still like to have dinner one night. Is there a night that you are free?"

"I'm sorry, Trevor," Meg said as she continued looking around her small house. "I should have been up front with you when we met. I just broke up with someone who I was involved with for a while. I'm just not ready to date right now."

"Too bad," he said in a whispered voice. It sent a chill through Meg. "It's much better when you choose to be my friend."

"What are you talking about?" Meg said looking out one of the kitchen windows.

"You'll see," he said as he hung up.

Meg set her cell phone down on an end table in the living room. From a distance, she heard the sound of glass breaking. She stood still listening to muffled sounds coming from the back of the house. Meg slowly began to walk toward the sound turning on lights. As she turned on the light in the little mudroom, a dark clad figure put a chloroformed soaked handkerchief over her mouth and nose. Meg struggled briefly and then slumped to the floor. Her assailant picked her up, carried her out the back door and into the woods.

CHAPTER 36

It was the middle of the night and the phone was ringing. Jake rolled over and moaned. He squinted at the clock as he reached for the phone and moaned again when he saw it was 2:15. He didn't get back from the Craig's until almost midnight.

"Hello," Jake mumbled as he answered the phone.

"Pastor Jake, I'm sorry to wake you."

Jake sat up trying to wake up more. "It's okay," he said as he tried to move Buddy over so he could get up.

"I'm Paul Stanwick, George's brother. He asked me to call you to let you know that the searchers found Kathy tonight."

"Where did they find her? Is she alright?" Jake asked immediately alert.

"It doesn't look too good. She's at the hospital right now. George asked me to call to see if you can get people to pray for her."

"Absolutely, I'll get our prayer chain going. Where was she found?"

"There were these caves deep in the woods. Some of the searcher thought that the missing kid might be there. In one of the caves, they found some camping stuff that looked like it belonged to the kid so they started searching all of them. Kathy was found left in one of them. She's really sick. The doctor says she had been drugged too."

"Has she been able to say what happened?"

"No, she's in a coma. She's so weak, I don't know if she can recover."

"Tell George that we're praying. Please call me if there is anything I or the church can do for you or George. I'll be sure to come over to the hospital too."

"That will mean a lot to George. You've done so much for him already. I'd better finish making calls."

"Okay. I'll see you tomorrow."

Jake hung up and said a quick prayer. Then he got up and went to his office to find Mrs. Baxter's home number. He found the number and made a quick call, promising to be at the office in the morning after he made a trip to Saratoga to visit Kathy. Jake found himself wide awake and just sat at his desk lost in thought. He hoped that Kathy being found was the start of things changing for the better.

Jake picked up his Bible and opened to the book of Psalms. As he read the familiar verses, he felt a nagging uncertainty, but forced it away so he could concentrate on the Word. As the Word began to capture his heart, Jake began to jot down a few notes on worship and praise. He loved the Psalms. So many times, Jake found a Psalm really spoke what he was feeling. David's love and trust in God was so evident to Jake and he longed to be "a man after God's own heart," just like David.

An hour later, Jake curled up on the couch and got a few hours of restful sleep. Buddy woke him up whining at the door. After waiting for him to come back in, Jake put on a CD of worship music and sang as he jumped in the shower. The shower invigorated him. He laughed when he went to get dressed at Buddy who was under the covers sound asleep.

As Jake poured his cup of coffee, the phone rang. "Hello," he answered.

"Good morning Jake, this is Millie."

"I hope its good news, Millie," Jake said as he took his coffee outside onto the deck. The sun had just come up over the tops of the trees and the sunrise was breathtaking.

"Oh, it is the best. We're coming home today!"

"That's great. How's Walt doing?"

"Well, of course, he will need some rehab and he still needs to take it easy for a couple of weeks. But just to have him home with me again will be wonderful."

"That's awesome. Now you make sure he doesn't over do it."

"Don't worry about that."

"I've got some good news too. Kathy Stanwick was found last night."

"Oh, Walt will be so happy to hear that. How is she?"

"She's at the hospital. She's not doing well physically, but she's been found."

"We will continue to pray for her. Let George know."

"I'll let him know when I get to the hospital this morning. I'll also let everyone know about Walt."

"I'll call Mrs. Baxter when we get back. I don't want her to feel that we've left her out."

Jake laughed, "She'll be happy to hear from you. Take care and tell Walt to take it easy."

"Okay, I'll talk to you later. Bye."

Jake hung up and shouted out the song that was playing in the house. He felt like rejoicing for these victories. As he watched the sun continue to climb over the trees, Jake felt peace for the first time in over a month.

CHAPTER 37

Sam longed to be outside away from the foul smells and the terror that he felt. When he finally came to after he fainted, he found he was in a different cage in a basement. He watched as Trevor went into a small room and Sam realized that there were women in there. Sam remembered hearing on the news that some women were missing. He never thought that Trevor could have been the person who took them. Sam was sure the one woman was dead, but then she moaned when Trevor nudged her with his foot.

Sam was alone for long periods of time when Trevor would leave. He knew where he was, in Trevor's basement. He knew the basement because he and Johnny had come in a bunch of times after Mr. Hanson had passed away. His family tried selling the house and rented it a few times when it didn't sell. Sam and Johnny wanted to snoop around and see if it was really haunted like a bunch of kids at school had said. But it was just an old house, and Sam lost interest.

Now he sat alone in the basement. He watched a few spiders climbing around. He usually was afraid of spiders, but not now. He heard noises overhead and knew that Trevor had come back. He also heard the sounds of the creature walking with him. Trevor came down and looked at Sam before going into a back room. The creature followed Trevor down the stairs and stared at Sam through the bars. Sam felt his heart begin to pound, but stared back.

The creature sighed and laid down. He put his head on his front paws and watched Sam. Sam sat on the blanket on the floor and felt really cold, but didn't move, just sat staring back. He noticed that the creature wasn't really that bad. He looked like a big wolf that Sam remembered seeing in a book. Although at night its eyes glowed, Sam noticed in day light they were just plain brown dog eyes. Maybe it was just a wolf with really long nails. The creature yawned showing Sam a mouth full of long razor sharp teeth. Sam knew this was no ordinary wolf, but something else.

Sam thought about Pastor Jake and wondered if God really did care about him like he had said. Sam bowed his head and began to pray. The creature narrowed its eyes and began to growl. Sam looked up and saw menace in its eyes, and he stopped praying. Sam thought that it wasn't possible that it knew he had been praying.

Sam decided to test it. He whispered, "Dear Jesus, help me please."

The creature got up and all the hair on its back stood on end. He snarled at Sam and paced over to the side of the cage that Sam was leaning against. Sam stood up and moved into the middle of the cage. Trevor came out of one of the back rooms. He said something in a foreign language, but the animal kept snarling. Trevor looked at Sam.

"What did you do?" he demanded.

"Nothing," Sam said in a quiet voice.

"It had to have been something. He knows that you are to be one with us now that Shamus is gone."

"Nothing," Sam said again. The creature began to calm down, but walked around the cage growling.

"It's alright," Trevor said to the creature. He went to it and began to pet its head. He kept talking to it quietly until it calmed down. Finally, it went back and laid down watching Sam again.

"Sit," Trevor said to Sam. Sam looked at Trevor and then sat on the cold cement. "Good. He needs to be sure of you if you want to stay alive. After all, he is a wild animal."

Sam felt himself trembling and closed his eyes. A low growl came from the creature and Sam looked up at it. Sam found he couldn't stare at it and just watched Trevor. He didn't know what Trevor was doing, but it was better than watching the wolf.

CHAPTER 38

Jake stood in front of the bookcase in Pastor Walt's office and started at the endless books trying to find some inspiration for a devotional for the men's breakfast that he was supposed to lead in the morning. After spending all day at the church office catching up on the piles of work that Mrs. Baxter had for him to do, Jake just couldn't seem to figure out what to say. Even though Jake realized that administrative work needed to be done, he felt like he wasted the day. He should have been at the Craig's looking for Sam, or at the hospital visiting Kathy and praying with George. Instead of helping two men in the congregation deal with difficulties in their lives, he was writing a thank you letter to the ladies' auxiliary for the fine dinner they put on last week. Mrs. Baxter insisted that these things needed to be done in a timely manner, especially since Jake had missed the dinner because he was out visiting.

Jake sighed feeling the burden of disapproval from Mrs. Baxter and the elders and wondered how they couldn't understand that the needs of the people outweighed the paperwork. Their disapproval was another reason Jake was doubting himself.

Turning away from the bookcase, Jake wandered into the sanctuary and stood in front of the pulpit. He looked down at the empty pews picturing the different people. After a few minutes, Jake walked off the platform and went to the pew that he usually sat in. Sitting down, he looked up at the big cross that was illuminated from behind. Jake bowed his head and began to pray. He began praying for the Craig's and then for other people in the congregation as their burdens lay heavy on Jake's heart. As he lost himself in prayer, Jake began to feel a Presence with him and all the stress and problems of the day began to fade.

After a while, Jake felt a hand on his shoulder and looked up. Pastor Walt stood beside him. "I remember many nights sitting just like you praying. A good place to be."

"Walt, you shouldn't..." Jake said starting to get up.

"Don't get up. Just move over," Walt said, sliding into the pew. He sat with a moan.

"You shouldn't be here," Jake tried to start again.

Walt waved him aside, "And where should I be? At home in bed? I've done enough of that. Besides nothing wrong with checking on a light in the church at night"

"I didn't mean to bother you."

"Oh, it doesn't bother me at all."

They sat in silence for a few minutes, each lost in thought. Finally, Walt said, "I've heard you've had your share of problems this past month."

Not sure how to respond, Jake just nodded. Walt went on, "running a church is a lot of responsibility especially when you don't have any experience. Now you take Mrs. Baxter. Sweet, sweet Christian lady, but definitely wants to see things run a certain way." Walt chuckled. "I sometimes think that God gave me Mrs. Baxter to teach me perseverance. I was kind of a procrastinator before she started working here."

Jake smiled, "Yeah, I know what you mean. But don't you think that writing letters and that kind of stuff isn't as important as counseling?"

"Everything has its place. Yes, it is a ministry and the people need to come first, but there is a place for writing letters and doing paperwork. It's finding the balance between going to someone's home and having them come to you."

Again they fell into a comfortable silence. Walt waited for Jake to say something. Finally Jake said, "I'm really worried about Sam Craig. He's missing again. He ran away the first time, just before his mother died. Stanley is so distraught. I feel that my words don't offer enough and my prayers seem ineffective to help the family."

"The Craigs have had some difficulties over the years for sure."

"I just felt like I should have been with Stanley today helping to look for Sam."

"I heard there were plenty of searchers."

"Then I should have gone the hospital with George."

"And what would that have accomplished? George has a lot of family to sit with him. He knows we care and will be praying for them."

Jake sat quietly contemplating what Walt said. Finally he said, "Reggie Bennett asked me to come back to the force."

"I know."

Jake looked at him surprised, "You know? How?"

Walt smiled, "I've got ways. People love to keep me informed of happenings."

"Did Reggie come to you?"

"No. Obviously you didn't go back. Why?"

"Why? I don't understand. Why would I even consider going back?"

"Was being on the force that bad?"

"No, I enjoyed being a cop, especially after I became a detective."

"And you were good at it too." Jake shrugged. "Yes, you were. You don't need to be ashamed. God gave you a gift."

"Okay, but I have responsibilities here."

"Especially with me laid up. Had the circumstances been different, would you have gone back to the force?"

"No," Jake said firmly. Walt waited for Jake to go on. "Well, not back to the force, but if I had the time, I might have tried to help. But yet, maybe not."

Walt nodded. "It's confusing to find your place, isn't it?

"Yes, it's just these particular crimes that have been happening. Everyone seems to think they are similar to some cases I had worked on years before. Part of me feels defensive because if this is the same perpetrator, then I really messed up sending an innocent man to jail...and Kathy wouldn't be in the hospital and these other women wouldn't be missing...."

"If you were wrong, it's not your fault, Jake. A jury found that man guilty, not you."

"But with evidence I obtained."

"Well, what about now?"

"What do you mean?"

"What are you going to do now? What has the Holy Spirit been prompting you to do?"

"That's the problem. I don't know."

"Sure you do. Think about it. Why are you in the ministry?"

"Because I want to help people really know the Lord."

"Something you couldn't do as a cop?"

"Not in the same way. I felt God leading me into the ministry. I had a yearning to teach, to reach the lost, to point people to a deeper commitment and relationship with Christ. Certainly nothing that I could do on the force. When

I sat and prayed with people the past few weeks, I knew I was in the heart of God's will. I couldn't solve their problems, but I pointed them to the One that could."

"Well, I should be getting back to the house or Millie will come after me," Walt said, chuckling. "I don't know who is harder on me, Millie or Mrs. Baxter. Now, you take a few days off from church work."

"Walt, I can't do that. The men's breakfast is in the morning…."

Walt stood and put his hand on Jake's shoulder. "I'll send Millie over with special directions for the elders. They can handle a breakfast. And I'll ask one of the elders to put together a special sermon for Sunday. I promise that I won't do anymore than Millie will let me and you promise to find Reggie and see if you can help in the investigation."

"I don't understand. Are you firing me?"

"Heavens no! There is such passion in you for the things of the Lord and for doing this work. You just need more experience, which is why I'm not ready to retire yet. But I know for a fact that the Granelle Police Department is in trouble. And I don't think that God would mind me loaning you to help. In fact, you'll be in a better place to pray for this town and for its people."

There was a soft sound in the foyer and both men turned to see Millie standing there with her arms crossed.

"See, what did I tell you," Walt whispered and then he said in a more serious tone, "on the night I had my heart attack, do you remember me telling you to get the prayer chain going?"

"Yes, I called and we all started to pray for you."

Millie came over and slipped her hand into Walt's. "It wasn't for me that I wanted the prayer for. It was for this town. That night, I was up late, just couldn't sleep. So, I paced around and prayed. I had a vision of a darkness coming into the town. I saw a creature that was just a dark shadow rush past the study window and its eyes glowed red in the darkness of the woods. I felt the evil. But before I could do anything, I had my heart attack, and then you know the rest."

"Walt, it wasn't a vision, it's real. My old partner told me that she's seen that creature and thinks it had to do with the disappearances."

"Millie, I think we need to pray for Jake before we go home. Is that okay?"

Millie nodded and reached out her other hand for Jake. Jake stood and the three bowed the heads and Walt prayed against the forces of evil.

CHAPTER 39

Jake woke up early the next morning. He hadn't slept much anyway. He was restless and couldn't wait to get to the police station and talk to Reggie. Having heard Walt talk about the dark creature, Jake knew that Meg had been right. He stopped at the station on the way home, but no one was there except the dispatcher. It was so late when he finally got home, he knew he'd have to wait until morning to talk to Reggie.

Jake took a long hot shower and dressed in jeans and a sweatshirt. It was a nice change from the dress slacks and shirts he had been wearing for the past month. He went to the kitchen and put on coffee. Since it was still too early to go to the station, Jake pulled out his Bible and opened it to Ephesians 5. Jake read, "For you were once in darkness, but now you are light in the Lord. Live as children of light (for the fruit of the light consists in all goodness, righteousness and truth) and find out what pleases the Lord. Have nothing to do with the fruitless deeds of darkness, but rather expose them. For it is shameful even to mention what the disobedient do in secret. But everything exposed by the light becomes visible, for it is light that makes everything visible." (NIV)

Jake sat rereading the passage and thinking about what Walt had said the night before about darkness coming to Granelle. He closed his eyes and prayed. The phone rang, interrupting his prayer. He got up and picked up the cordless that was on the counter.

"Jake, this is Millie." Jake's heart jumped at the sound of her voice. "Nothing's wrong. But Walt and I were just sitting here reading the Bible together. Walt wanted me to call you and tell you to read Ephesians 5. He said that you need to expose the deeds of the darkness. Does that make sense to you?"

"Absolutely, I was just reading the same passage in the Bible when you called."

"We are praying for you, Jake. Be careful."

"I will, and tell Pastor Walt thank you for me."

"Call us later. I don't want Walter to worry about you."

"Okay. Talk to you later then. Bye."

Jake hung up the phone and looked at the time. Even though it was still early, Jake decided to go to the station and see what he could figure out on his own. He stopped and filled the water and food bowls for Buddy figuring he wouldn't be back for awhile.

Half an hour later, Jake pulled into the parking lot at the police station. He parked his pickup next to a car and sat for a few minutes listening to the ticking of the engine as it cooled. It had been a long time since he had done any police work and he felt excited and nervous about the possibility of working on the force, even temporarily. Jake even wondered if he could work with Meg again. Finally, he got out figuring at least he could begin to make a list of what he knew so that Reggie or Meg could fill in the gaps.

The dispatcher looked up in surprise as Jake walked in. "Hi, Jake," Trudy said. "No one here but me right now."

"That's okay," he replied. "I'm finally free to help out in the investigation. So, I thought I'd get started."

"Captain Bennett will be glad to hear that. I've been working dispatch, so there's not much I can tell you. The captain should be here in about an hour or so."

"That's fine. I'll just find a desk and get started with what I already know."

Jake walked into the squad room and looked around. He walked around the room trying to find a place to sit and work. Finally, he settled on Meg's desk since it was the only uncluttered desk in the room. He opened the drawers and found them empty, except for a few pens. Jake grabbed a pen and then went over to another desk and took a legal pad.

Jake sat and began to list the names of the victims and what he knew about them. He worked for a while developing a list and realized just how much he didn't know. Jake finally turned on the computer that was on the desk and waited while it booted up. He glanced over at the door to see if Trudy was watching him. Finally, Jake sat looking at the log in screen for the police force. As the cursor blinked, Jake decided to try his old badge number and password. But found his access denied.

Jake got up and went to the break room. He looked in the cabinets and was surprised to find everything just where it was a few years ago. He rinsed out the coffee pot and made a fresh pot. While the coffee was being made, he stood looking at the vending machine trying to figure out if he was hungry. Shrugging, he turned away and opened the cupboard and found two mugs. Jake filled them with the fresh coffee and went out to the dispatcher desk to find it empty.

Jake set the cups on the desk and called out for Trudy, listening as his voice echoed in the empty building. He looked out the door at the parking lot where his truck sat alone. He saw that dust was blowing across the parking lot like a car had just driven on it. The phone on the desk rang and Jake turned and looked at it. He went over to the desk and pushed the button for the ringing line.

"Granelle Police Department," Jake answered.

"Well, Preacher…looks like you changed sides," the voice whispered.

Jake pushed the record button on the phone and said, "Don't make assumptions about things you don't know anything about."

"Ah, but I already know that you failed as a preacher. I've been watching while you ran all over town making fool out of yourself. So you came back to crime fighting where you already were a failure," the whispered voice practically hissed.

"What makes you think that?" Jake wanted to just hang up, but knew that he had to keep him talking so that he might be able to get some clues.

"Everyone knows you're a failure. Oh, the dispatcher…what's her name? Oh yes, Trudy, will be my next victim. I've been waiting for you to come back to play with me, Jake." The line went dead.

Jake hung up the phone and looked back out the front door. He hoped to see something, but didn't. He walked down the empty hall to the supply room hoping that everything was still in the same place there. He found the key to the gun cabinet hidden on the little ledge over the chalkboard. Unlocking the cabinet, he pulled out a service revolver and put a round of bullets in it. He put some extra shells in his front pocket. Slipping the revolver into his waistband, Jake relocked the cabinet and stuck the key back.

Jake went through the squad room to Reggie's office knowing he would have a clear view of the parking lot. He looked out into the parking lot and his truck was still the only vehicle there. Jake then went over to Reggie's desk and looked up his phone number.

CHAPTER 40

Less than an hour later, Jake, Reggie, Pete, and Greg sat around Reggie's desk listening to the recorded conversation for the fourth time. Reggie shook his head.

"Can't tell too much from this. I'll send it down to Marty and see if he can get any background noise from it," Reggie said.

"Sounds like he's got a foreign accent or something," Jake said.

"Hey, that guy that picked up that girl at the bar was supposed to have a foreign accent," Pete said. He picked up a folder on the desk and started looking through it. Reggie stopped him.

"Don't waste your time. The guy did have a foreign accent, according to the roommate. Besides, we already are making the assumption that this is our guy," Reggie looked at Jake. "So, do I get to give you back your badge? We need the help. Aside from Marty, you're now looking at the whole force."

Jake nodded, "Temporarily, at least. Pastor Walt is home and he is going to run the church through his wife and the elders for a few days." Reggie grunted. "Look Reggie...umm...Captain, I want to help out anyway I can. But my heart is in the church. Besides, Meg will be back next week and we'll get Trudy back too."

Greg shifted nervously and Pete cleared his throat, but neither said anything. Jake looked at them confused. Reggie leaned back in his chair and it groaned under his weight. "Problem is Riley was supposed to show up for work on Monday. It's now Wednesday, and I haven't heard from her."

"Have you tried to reach her?"

"Is that my job? I don't think so. She took a mandatory vacation and was told to report to me at 9:00 Monday morning. She's not here, so she's gone."

"Are you kidding me?" Reggie looked like he was going to explode, so Jake went on quickly. "Did she talk to you the other day like I told her to?"

"Talk to me about what?"

"Meg came to my place. She said that she met this guy at Joe's and he seemed to be fixated on her. She thought this could be the man, especially since he has some type of large dog that looks like a wolf. He knew where she was staying in Granelle."

Reggie stared intently at Jake. "She was working on this case last week? Is that what you're telling me, Peterson?"

"What I'm telling you is that she came to me afraid of some creep and was afraid to go to you. I'm not trying to disrespect you, but if Meg has a possible suspect in her sights and has information about him having some dog, there is a connection to at least the Stanwick case. I saw a large animal in the woods that morning when I left the Stanwicks. Meg told me there were hairs at the scene."

"Okay, let me catch you up on Riley's theory. She believes that there is a werewolf in Granelle. Let me tell you what I know. Kathy Stanwick is in a coma suffering from severe dehydration, starvation, and a lethal mix of narcotics. There were no bite marks and no animal hairs. We have yet to find Lauren Thomas, Sam Craig, or Martha Rowley. And to add to that list, my dispatcher has been kidnapped, apparently by someone who wants to play games with you."

"And I'm sure there's a lot more that I don't know that you can fill me in on. But I do know that Riley has a possible suspect. Even if she is out of the department, we need to find out who this man is and interrogate him. Find out if there is a connection to all these cases. Her approach is off, I'll grant you that, but maybe she has the right suspect."

"I don't have time for you to be running around behind Riley cleaning up her mess. If you want to come back to the force, you will work with Matthews and follow up on the leads we have. Do I make myself clear?"

Jake sat back in his chair and looked at Pete and Greg. Neither would meet his eye and both sat staring at the floor. Jake shrugged and stood. "What I thought was, you wanted my help. I have more police experience than anyone in this room besides you. But ultimately, it's your choice if I work on the force or not. Meg thought this man was after her and it terrified her. Do you know if anyone has heard from her?" Jake looked at Pete who shook his head and then to Reggie who didn't respond. "You know what I told her Reggie, I told her that her theory had flaws and she was letting her bias interfere with her ability to see the case clearly."

Jake turned and walked to the door. When he got to the door Reggie said, "So what was the flaw?"

"What?" Jake said turning back around.

"What was the flaw in her theory?"

"Kathy Stanwick. She told me that this man was after single women. In the Angelos case, all four of those women were single. And from what I know about Thomas and Rowley, they were single. But Kathy is married."

"But out of all those woman, Stanwick was the only one whose been found. We've always assumed the others were deceased, but have no real evidence that they are."

"Okay, so was Kathy dumped because she was married? Are the others missing because they are single?"

Reggie shrugged, "Maybe."

"I just realized something," Pete said interrupting. "Trudy makes number four."

"What do you mean?" Reggie asked.

"In the old cases, there were four missing women. If we eliminate Stanwick because she was married and she's been found, we have four missing women again…Rowley, Thomas, Meg, and now Trudy. Four. Does that mean anything?"

"First of all, Riley isn't missing. Second, you forgot Sam Craig. How would he fit into the puzzle? Three missing women and one boy." Reggie said shaking his head.

Jake walked back to the desk. "What a minute. Maybe you've got something. I know you don't want to go over what Meg was working on…but she mentioned something about a ritual. Maybe it takes four women. And maybe Sam takes Angelos place this time. By the time we picked up Angelos, he was so insane we couldn't even get anything competent out of him. Didn't you say he wanted to talk to me last week?"

Reggie nodded, "Yeah, but it's too late. He's gone again under heavy sedation, talking about creatures in the night, same as the last time."

"Reggie, we've got to at least see if Meg's alright and figure out who this man is."

Reggie sighed and shifted in the seat again. "I don't like this. Take Matthews with you, but you find her and bring her to me. I'll interview her."

"Sure," Jake said lightheartedly.

"Peterson, I mean it. I'll interview her." Jake turned to leave with Greg following him. "Hold on Peterson." Jake turned back and Reggie held out a badge to him. "Better make this official and sign out the gun from Driscole before you leave the station. I don't want any legal headaches after we put this guy away."

CHAPTER 41

Greg drove slowly down Consul Road looking for Meg's car in the driveways. Since it was a weekday, most cars were gone and the houses empty.

"This isn't getting us anywhere," Jake finally said. "Pull over a minute. There's a car in that driveway." Greg pulled the car to the side of the road and Jake got out. He walked to the house and rang the doorbell. Jake looked back at Greg who sat waiting in the car. Finally an older man came to the door, still in his pajamas. He just stared through the glass. Jake showed him his badge. The man cracked opened the storm door.

"I'm sorry to bother you. I'm Detective Peterson. I'm looking for a house that was for rent here in the last week or so. Can you tell me which one it was?"

"House for rent? That would be the Johnson house. The small blue house with the white shutters about five houses up on the right. Can't miss it. He moved south after his wife passed away. But couldn't sell the place…guess he decided to rent it."

Jake nodded, "Thanks for your help."

"There some problem that I should know about. Vandals or something?"

"No, nothing to worry about, sir. We're just looking for a colleague."

"Oh, a cop moved in up the street." He looked pleased.

"Well, thanks for the help. Can I stop by again if I have any other question?"

"Sure, sure. Name's James Southold."

"Thanks again, Mr. Southold. "

Jake walked down the steps. "You tell that cop to stop over when he gets settled. Like to talk about some kids that need a talking to up the street."

"Okay, I'll mention it to her."

"Her?" The old man muttered something Jake didn't hear as he walked back to the car. He got back in and directed Greg up the road. Mr. Southold stood on the porch watching them pull into the driveway of the rental house.

Jake got out and waved at him and he went back into his house with a disgusted look on his face.

"What was that all about?" Greg asked.

"Didn't like it that I told him the new cop in his neighborhood was a her," Jake said amused. Jake rang the doorbell and looked in the window. He could see boxes sitting in the living room. Jake waited a few minutes and then tried the door and found it was locked.

"Now what?" Greg asked.

"Let's try the back door." Greg followed Jake around the house. It was a small house and the yard hadn't been cleared in a long time. The tangled dead grass was full of leaves and the side of the house was almost impossible to get through. But Jake pushed his way through. The backyard was in just as bad condition. Jake stopped at the back door and looked down at the broken door frame. He reached in the pocket of his jacket and pulled out gloves. As he put them on, he looked through a side window and couldn't see anything through the dirt and grime.

"You really think Riley moved into this dump?"

"I don't know. But someone broke into this house regardless if Meg lives here or not. You better radio this in and get someone from the department out here."

"Why? We're here."

Jake looked down at Greg realizing how inexperienced he really was. "We don't have any equipment to process the scene for forensic evidence. I have probable cause to go in to be sure there are no victims needing medical assistance. But beyond that, we don't want to destroy any evidence. So, go radio this in."

Greg left to go back to the car as Jake pushed gently on the door. He pulled his gun out and carefully stepped into the mud room. Jake quickly searched the house and found it empty. But everything was a mess. Boxes were half empty and everything was placed haphazardly around the small house. Plates and utensils were on a table in the living room, curtains were in a pile on the floor, and everything was dirty. The windows were streaked with dirt and the carpeting was stained and grimy. Jake couldn't believe Meg would move into a place like this.

Less than an hour later, Jake waited in the front yard while Driscole and Reggie began to process the scene. He was impatient to see if he could find any clues that Meg had on the case. He had already tried calling Meg's parents and a few other people he remembered. But he only talked to one friend who hadn't heard from Meg in over a month.

"Peterson," Reggie called Jake from the front door. "Driscole may have found some evidence that you may need."

Jake eagerly went back into the house. Reggie took him to the kitchen and showed him an overstuffed expandable file. Jake pulled out a few of the sheets and saw Kathy Stanwick's name. Jake looked around the cluttered mess looking for any evidence. On the table was Meg's purse and Reggie had already carefully gone through it. He found her cell phone on the end table and flipped it opened. The screen showed that her voice mail was full. With his pen, Reggie pushed a few buttons to show missed calls going back to Friday. He closed the phone and put it on the table.

"I don't like this, Peterson," Reggie said in a gruff voice.

"Me either," Jake said as he looked inside a box full of papers on the table. He lifted a few of the top papers to see what they were and found some grocery lists and bills. He looked at the familiar handwriting and put the papers on the table. Looking through the box, he found just a bunch of personal papers, letters, bills, and bank statements. "Can I take this file back to the precinct?" Jake asked.

"You can take it, but keep in mind what we've talked about. Riley wasn't herself the past few weeks. Just look at this place," Reggie said gesturing at the mess. "Would she really have rented this place if she was acting like herself?"

"I don't know. She may have been desperate. Or maybe she thought it had some potential."

Reggie made a disgusted sound. "You better get moving. We're losing another day fast."

"Okay. Do you know where Matthews is?"

"I think he's in the backyard. There are some strange animal footprints. Driscole is getting an imprint of it."

"Animal? Like maybe dog prints?"

"Looks too big to be a dog print." Jake looked at Reggie in surprise. "Don't say it. Just get going. There's a lot of stuff to check out yet. We'll be back at the station as soon as we finish up here." Jake nodded and left to find Greg.

CHAPTER 42

Greg drove back to the station while Jake sat reading through Meg's file. He could see there were similarities between the older cases and the two new ones. But there were obvious differences as well, especially if he counted Meg and Trudy. Jake was puzzled by all of the references to animal hairs that Meg had through her papers. Her scrawled notes about a Dr. Chevers were practically illegible. Jake began to methodically sort through the messy papers, separating what he believed was real evidence from conjecture.

As the car pulled into the station, Jake found the name of Shamus O'Leary. He read Meg's notes: foreigner, dog, rental, and loner. "Hey, Greg, does the name Shamus O'Leary mean anything to you?" Jake asked.

"No, haven't heard of him. Anything in that mess?" Greg asked as he stopped the car.

"Not really. Maybe a few leads. We need to make some calls and get some direction. Here's a list of contacts Bennett pulled off from Meg's phone. You try calling this list and see when any of these people last heard from her. I've got a few other leads to follow."

Pete was sitting at the dispatcher desk on the phone and nodded to Jake as he walked in. Jake went to the squad room and went right to Meg's desk.

After a few hours, Jake was tired from reading and finding no answers. Meg's notes had gotten harder to follow at the end and much of what she wrote didn't make sense. She had notes on creatures and pictures from the Internet on demons and werewolves. It was hard for Jake to separate the facts of the cases from the fiction. He kept praying for God to show him the answers, but so far, nothing was coming to him. Reggie came back from the house and walked up to Jake.

"Anything yet?" he asked.

"No. Most of this is just a mess," Jake said gesturing at the papers scattered across the desk. "The early notes around the Rowley and Stanwick cases are neat and the way I remember Meg's work. But then it goes off track. This morning, this all sounded logical. Now I understand where you were coming from."

"So where does this leave us? What does your gut tell you, Jake?"

"To find a wastepaper basket and start over again. But I know we are running out of time. I wish there was something to salvage here," Jake shook his head. "But there is little help. The forensics isn't helping either. The only place I have any evidence is in the Stanwick case, but that case is different because Kathy was found."

Reggie sat down in the chair next to the desk. "Well, the stuff that I went through pretty much is the same as what you've seen. A lot of notes that make no sense. Threads of her theory about creatures and werewolves…"

"That's part of the problem, too. Pastor Ryerson saw that creature."

"Jake…," Reggie said in a cautious tone.

"The night he had his heart attack, he saw that creature run past his window. He told me about it last night. It matched the description of the animal that Meg told me about. That stuff isn't in this file. Let's go off that theory. Someone has a big wolf and is using it to scare women. Maybe he uses it to scare them and then he pretends to be this hero rescuing them, but he abducts them…see where I'm going?"

"Sort of. But how does that explain Trudy."

"Trudy is personal. I'm here and that doesn't make that man happy. Maybe I got too close last time. Maybe he even planted the evidence that I found that convicted Angelos because I got too close. We just wanted someone to blame. Now he wants to toy with me a little to throw me off balance. So I run off wasting time like I did this morning."

"I really wish that Mrs. Stanwick would wake up so we could question her."

"I pray she wakes up, but that's because I want her to be okay. I can't get past the question of how this happened. Did this man pick them up? Does he lure them out and get the wolf to scare them?"

"This is conjecture."

"Not really. Meg came to my house last week. She had seen the creature in her yard at Consul Road. Who's to say that when Lauren left the bar that night that the wolf was in the parking lot and that person led her to a place to "protect" her?"

"Well, that would make some sense. But again, this is all speculative. Where is your evidence? Who is this person?"

"I'm not going to find that answer here. Meg mentioned a name, but I didn't really pay attention. But she met some guy at Joe's, and Lauren met some guy at a bar. No one knows anything about Martha. And I can't seem to get Sam Craig out of my mind, either. Guess it's time for me to get out of here and make some house calls. And I'll check out the roommate that reported Lauren missing."

"Okay, I'll have Marty pull all the cases, even the old ones to see if there is any forensics in all these cases that match. It's getting late, we are losing another day."

They both got up and went in opposite directions. Jake motioned to Greg who followed him out of the building.

CHAPTER 43

Meg squinted as the door opened, spilling light into the small room she was in. She had slept so much in the last few days that she was disoriented as to time and days. She knew that the food she had been given had to be drugged from the dry mouth and the groggy feeling she always seemed to have. She hoped that by now, she had been missed by someone. Meg heard a tin plate slide on the floor, and she was once again engulfed in darkness.

Meg closed her eyes. The smell of the food made her feel hungry. She lay on the bare mattress and listened to the silence. Her stomach growled and Meg tried to fight off the feelings knowing that if she ate, she would just go back to sleep. She tried to focus on something other than hunger, but couldn't. She rolled over restless and thought she heard a sound. She lay still listening and heard a scrapping sound again.

Meg sat up and felt dizzy. She sat still with her eyes closed and heard a soft muffled sound. Groping around in the darkness, she felt the cold cement wall next to her. She crept along the wall until she reached a corner. She continued to go down the next wall until she felt the door. Meg tried to adjust her eyes to the darkness and finally noticed a dark grey line at the bottom of the door. She felt around on the floor until she reached the plate of food. Pushing it out of her way, Meg laid flat on the floor and tried to see under it. She could only make out a little of the cement floor beyond the door. She put her ear to the crack and listened. She could hear soft crying.

Putting her mouth near the crack, she called out, "Hello?" She could still hear the soft crying. "Hello is someone there?" she said louder.

"Who's there?" she heard almost in a whisper.

"This is Det. Riley from the Granelle Police Department. Who are you?"

"My name is Lauren. Help me, please, before he comes back," the voice said louder and more excited.

"Lauren? Lauren Stewart?"

"Yes, that's me."

"Lauren, you need to listen to me. Don't eat the food. It's drugged."

"Just get me out of here."

Meg sighed feeling sick to her stomach. "Lauren, I'm locked in here too."

"NO," Lauren screamed and started crying again.

"Lauren." Meg waited for a response. But the girl just kept crying. "Lauren, are you listening to me?"

There was no reply. Meg closed her eyes. "She's not listening, but I am," another voice said closer to her.

"Who is this?" Meg asked.

"My name is Sam. The food he gives me isn't drugged though. But I've watched him put the drugs in yours."

"Sam? Do you know how many of us are down here?"

"Well, besides you and me, there's the girl who is always crying. Then there's this other lady. But she hasn't been eating and she hasn't made much noise in the last few days."

"So that's four of us?"

"No, there's five. He brought another older lady down here this morning. She's been asleep all day."

"Sam, how do you know all this? Are you locked in?"

"I'm in a cage, not locked behind doors like you. Are you really a cop?"

"Yes, I am. Don't you remember me? I was one of the detectives that searched for you."

"I'm scared."

"I know Sam. I'm scared too. But I'm going to try to get us out of here."

Sam laughed bitterly. "You think so? You haven't seen the things I've seen."

Meg felt a wave of nausea hit her. She lay still for a few minutes just listening to Lauren crying. Finally she said, "Sam, its Trevor who's doing this, isn't it."

"Yeah. I thought he was my friend. I think he killed my mom."

Meg was about to say something when she heard footsteps over head.

"That's him coming back to get the plates," Sam said. "You better get away from the door because the wolf will be with him."

Meg shuttered and crept back to the mattress. She lay with her back to the door. Away from the door, everything was muffled and Meg couldn't make out what was being said. When her door opened and the light poured in, Meg kept her eyes closed as if she was sleeping. She heard Trevor walk over to her and nudge her with his foot. Meg groaned softly and heard a growl near the door. Trevor walked back toward the door and picked up the plate. He hesitated.

"Don't try anything stupid, Detective Riley. I'd hate to have to kill you before I'm ready." When Meg didn't move or respond, Trevor went out and slammed the door. Meg heard the key lock in the door and realized that was the first time she had heard that sound. She turned her face into the musty mattress, feeling like a fool.

A few moments later, Sam called out to her. "Hey, did you hear me?"

"What did you say?" Meg called out trying to pull herself together.

"I said, I didn't know you weren't locked in. That means the other women probably aren't locked in either."

Meg sat up slowly trying not to get too dizzy and crept back to the door. "Sam, can you repeat what you just said."

"I don't think any of the other women are locked in."

"Have you talked to anyone besides me?"

"No, I've been too afraid to."

"Okay. Do you have any way of knowing when Trevor leaves?"

"Usually I can hear him going out. But I know he is planning on doing the ritual soon. So I don't know if he will go out again."

"The ritual?"

"Yeah, he said it will make me one of the keepers."

Meg tried to remember what Dr. Chevers had told her about the rituals, but she found it hard to focus with the drugs still in her system. But there was something important she needed to remember.

"Detective Riley?" Sam said in a quiet voice.

"Why don't you just call me Meg?"

"Okay...I've been sitting in here thinking a lot about all the things that have happened lately and all the things that I've done. I didn't really get lost, I ran away because I was mad about stuff."

When he stopped, Meg said, "I figured that."

"You did? Then why didn't you say anything to my Dad?"

"Because your mother was found and I figured you and your father had enough to deal with."

"Thanks for not telling him…." Sam hesitated. "Meg, do you think God loves me?"

Meg closed her eyes and sighed. "I don't know much about God, Sam," she replied.

"I was just wondering because I did some bad stuff. At my mom's funeral, I was crying and stuff. Pastor Jake came over to me and put his arm around me. He said that God loves me even though I ran away. That I just needed to ask God to forgive me. But I was mad at God, you know? I was mad because my Mom died, because Ted got Melinda to be his girlfriend, and now I was going to have to move away. But now I'm really scared. I keep praying, but I think God is mad at me now because no one is coming to rescue me."

"Well, like I said, I don't know about God, but I'm here. I think I've got an idea to get us out of here."

"I don't think you can get us out," Sam said dejected. "I see stuff and that creature…," Sam shuddered. "He's awful, he's mean, and he stinks. He looks right into my eyes and I feel like it is the most evil thing in the world. When I pray, it's like he knows because he growls at me."

"Trust me. I'll find a way to get us out."

"I wish Pastor Peterson was here. Every time, he sees me, he tells me that God loves me and he is praying for me and my family. Plus someone told me he used to be a cop. I'd feel safe if he was here because he's got it all covered. Do you know him? Was he really a cop?"

"Yes, I know him and he was a cop before he got religious."

Not hearing the sarcasm in her voice, Sam went on. "That's neat. Do you think God will tell Pastor Jake where we are so he can come save us?"

"I don't think it works that way."

"Oh," Sam said sadly.

Meg felt a stab of guilt, but shrugged it off. "Look, I need to go back to sleep for a while, Sam. The drug isn't worn off yet. But yell really loud when you hear Trevor leave. Then we'll work on getting us out of here. Okay?"

"Sure," Sam said. "But if it's alright with you, I think I'll still pray and ask God to save us too."

"Sure, whatever makes you feel better," Meg said. She wasn't really planning on sleeping. She just didn't want to hear anymore about Jake and God right now. She needed to make a plan and to remember what Dr. Chevers had said about the ritual so that she could get them out alive.

CHAPTER 44

The house calls the day before provided nothing new, except that no one had heard or seen Meg in a week. Jake kept thinking that maybe Sam was somehow connected. At the early morning meeting, Reggie sent everyone in opposite directions again. Reggie was going to talk to Mo Reynolds, and Pete was heading down to Albany to talk to Dr. Chevers. Jake insisted that he go to the Craigs, even though Reggie felt that Jake should be going to Albany. Jake had a feeling that maybe Sam had said something to Stanley that would help.

Jake knocked on the Craig's door and waited. Greg shifted next to him. "I still don't know why we came here. The Captain wanted to send us to Albany," he said. "I know we talked this morning about Sam maybe being a part of this whole thing, but the kid ran away before. I think this is a waste of time."

Jake looked at Greg and nodded. "I can understand why you'd think that. If it was four years ago, I'd probably think the same thing. But I've been really praying about this, and I just kept feeling like God is leading me here. I know you probably won't understand that."

Greg shrugged, "Guess that's why you left the force. Can't go on 'feelings.'"

"Maybe you're right, Greg. But I also have about ten years of experience in investigating, too. Sometimes, even a cop follows his instincts."

Greg muttered something Jake didn't understand as Stanley opened the door. He looked like he had aged overnight. Jake noticed grey hair that he hadn't seen before and he looked exhausted.

"Oh, Pastor Jake, I wasn't expecting you," Stanley said and then noticed Greg. He clutched the door frame. "No, please don't tell me that Sam is dead, too."

Jake reached out and put his hand on Stanley's shoulder. "No. It's not that at all. Pastor Walt is loaning me out to the police force. So, I'm here as a detective trying to find Sam and the women who are missing. Can we come in and ask you a few questions?"

Stanley sagged against Jake and nodded. They walked into the living room that was piled with shipping boxes. Clothes were all over the couch. Stanley walked past the mess and led them to the kitchen. Even there, dishes and food were half packed and sitting on the counters and table. Stanley put a bunch of pots on top of some boxes and sat down. As Jake sat, he felt deep compassion for Stanley.

"Stanley, when was the last time you got some sleep, or even ate something?" Jake asked.

"Doesn't matter. Pastor Jake, I just don't understand how God could have allowed this to happen. First Clara and now Sam," he lowered his head and a tear dropped on his hand.

"Stanley, you know that evil exists in this world. We just have to keep praying for Sam."

Greg cleared his throat. Jake looked up at him and just shook his head a little bit. Stanley kept looking down shaking his head. "It feels like it's no use. My sister called and said that I should just leave. But how can I leave until I know if Sam…"

"You're right. You can't leave yet. There are so many unanswered questions and you might have some of those answers."

Stanley finally looked up at Jake. His eyes were tear stained and red. "I don't know any more than I've already told the officers before."

"Well there is something new. I had a talk with Pastor Walt. He told me that the night he had his heart attack, he saw a dark animal run past his study window. He said that it had eyes that glowed red in the darkness. Have you seen an animal like that out here?"

"Animal?" Stanley said his forehead creasing. "There was something…." Stanley got up and walked down the hall. Jake and Greg followed him. He searched around his desk and then began to pull out boxes.

"Stanley, what are you looking for?" Jake asked.

"I looked up something on the Internet about animals that had eyes like that. I found something." Stanley put a large box on his desk and began to rifle through the papers. "The night that Sam got into all that trouble, he was late coming home from school. After Clara went to bed, Sam asked me about what would make an animal's eyes glow in the darkness."

"This is really important," Jake said. "What did Sam say about it?"

Stanley stopped for a minute. "He said it scared him. I know he was scared because he was crying. It's not like Sam to cry even when he gets in trouble. Clara never let him cry. She said he needed to be a little man." Stanley shook his head and started going through the box again.

Jake reached out and stopped him. "I need to know more about that night. Several people have seen this animal… I think I saw that animal the night that Kathy Stanwick disappeared."

Stanley hesitated for a minute letting that sink in. He nodded and sank down into the desk chair. "Sam was late getting home from school. We knew that the principal had purposely kept him after school, but even so with it getting dark so early, we…I was nervous about how dark it was getting. Sam finally came in at dusk. He looked scared and nervous. I guess I took it for the trouble he had in school that day. You remember that day, don't you?"

"Yes, it was the day after Pastor Walt's heart attack."

"Yeah, that's right. Then you came out the next day when Sam got lost in the woods."

"But what happened that night?"

"Sam asked me if an adult could stop a wild animal from attacking. I told him probably not. Then he asked me about the eyes glowing. I told him not to go into the woods until I had a chance to check around and ask Trevor about the animal."

"Trevor?"

"Yes, he is our neighbor down the road. Hmm, I guess that's sort of when we met him. He told me he had a dog that was kind of mean."

"Did you ever see the dog?"

"No, I never did."

"If he's your neighbor, how come you just met him?"

"Oh, he said he rented the old Hanson place for track season in Saratoga. I guess he did that one other time, too. He likes Granelle so much he decided to stay for a while."

"Stanley, this is really important," Jake started, but was interrupted by his cell phone ringing. He looked at the caller ID and handed the phone to Greg. Greg stepped into the hall and answered it.

"Pastor Jake, I don't really see what Trevor's dog has to do with all this. What does the dog have to do with Sam missing?"

"There is, apparently, some connection to a wolf type animal in these cases. What did you find out on the Internet about the animals?"

"Now it seems a little foolish," he said with a shrug. "It was something about werewolves and old folklore."

"Did Trevor ever say where he was from?"

"No, somewhere overseas. He has a foreign accent."

"Excuse me," Greg said from the door. "Jake, Bennett has some information he wants to talk to us about."

"Hold on one minute. The Hanson place, that's at the end of your road?"

"Yes, the old one at the dead end. It just sits in the woods really. After meeting Trevor, I was surprised he really likes living there. When old Mr. Hanson died five years ago, it was a dump then. Trevor has been the only one who has ever rented it. Maureen is the real estate agent for the family."

"Thanks, Stanley. Don't give up hope. Just keep on praying for Sam. If you find those articles, call me. I'm still interested."

"Sure, sure." Stanley went back to looking in the box while Jake followed Greg out.

"Bennett's annoyed that you didn't answer your phone," Greg said once they got outside. "He wants us back at the station, pronto."

"We'll go back after we visit Stanley's neighbor."

Jake walked to the driver's side and put his hand out for the key. Greg shook his head. "No way. Bennett said to come back to the station."

"Look, we are here right now. I just want to meet this man and see his dog. Trevor was the name of the man that Meg mentioned to me. What if this is the same guy...he may be our suspect."

Greg looked doubtful as he got in the car. Jake pulled the car out of the driveway and headed toward the dead end.

CHAPTER 45

Jake stepped off the porch and walked to the corner of the old house. He looked down the short driveway to the old garage that stood empty. He saw the tail end of a car sticking out behind the house. Walking back to the porch, he glanced in the window into the empty living room. Somewhere from inside, they heard a growl. Jake looked at Greg uncomfortably.

Trevor opened the door leaving the screen door between them. "May I help you?"

"Sir, we are from the Granelle Police Department. I'm Greg Matthews and this is my partner, Jake Peterson. We are investigating the recent disappearances in the area and were wondering if we could ask you a few questions."

"I'd be glad to help in any way I can. I am friends with the Craigs and have been helping in the search for the young boy. But I'm afraid now isn't a convenient time. Perhaps, tomorrow I can…"

"I'm sorry," Jake said interrupting. "But we don't really have time to wait. There are several women in our community that are missing and, of course, the Craig boy."

Trevor looked annoyed, "I'm sorry to ask, but do you have any identification?"

Greg and Jake showed him their badges. Trevor stared knowingly at Jake. "You must have a brother, officer."

"No," Jake said shaking his head as he put his badge away.

"Then it was you that performed Mrs. Craig's funeral?"

Jake nodded and then realized that Trevor was the stranger he had seen by the cars. "Yes, I did and I remember seeing you there. Why didn't you join the rest of the mourners?"

"Well, I don't think I really need to answer questions posed to me by a preacher. So, if you don't mind, I have other things to do."

"Well, I do mind. See I'm back on the police force."

"How convenient. Don't know which side to play for...preacher?"

"So have you made any anonymous phone calls lately? See, your voice sounds familiar. Not everyone in Granelle has an accent like yours."

Trevor chuckled. He turned and started closing the door. Jake reached out and opened the screen.

Greg made a noise behind him and whispered, "Jake, by the book. Let's come back with a search warrant."

Trevor and Jake glared at each other. Jake sent up a silent prayer. In the stillness of the moment, Jake heard a soft noise from inside the house.

"I am sorry." Jake said, putting his hand up and Trevor started closing the door. "It's just that I'm concerned. Two of the missing women work for the police department. Are you aware of that?"

"No, how would I know that?" Trevor said frowning.

"Look, I know you are busy. But Mr. Craig mentioned that Sam was afraid of some type of a dog in the area. He also mentioned that you own a dog. Was Sam afraid of your dog?"

Something dark passed over Trevor's eyes and for a moment, Jake thought he looked mean. "No, Sam is not afraid of my dog. Excuse me, I really need to get moving."

Jake sighed as the door slammed. With nothing he could do, Jake followed Greg back to the car.

CHAPTER 46

Sam heard the door slam and huddled under the dirty blanket. The creature laid next to his cage with his head on his paws. Trevor came down the stairs and glared at Sam. He walked to a back room and came out with a black duffle bag.

"So, you talked about him," Trevor said motioning to the creature. The creature lifted its head and looked at Sam.

"What do you mean?" Sam asked in a whisper, fear flooded him.

"Don't play stupid, kid," Trevor yelled. "I told you that he wouldn't hurt you if you were my friend, didn't I?" Sam trembled and pulled the blanket closer. Trevor set the bag down and walked to the cage. Grabbing two bars, he yelled again. "Do you have any idea what you did? Now that preacher is on to me. Perhaps I was wrong about you."

The creature growled. Sam looked up and saw that the creature was looking at Trevor. "I'm sorry, Trevor," Sam said softly. The creature looked Sam right in the eyes, as if understanding. "It was the first night when I met you. I was scared."

"Too late to be sorry. If only Shamus was still here, he would know what to do."

Trevor dropped his hands and picked up the duffle bag again. He walked over to a bench and started putting items into the bag. Sam continued to watch the creature. The creature got up and stretched. He walked around the cage to the corner where Sam was huddled. He stuck his muzzle between the bars. Sam reached out his hand and gently touched the soft muzzle. With his hand shaking, Sam began to pet its nose. Deliberately, the creature nipped Sam's finger. Jerking his hand away, Sam looked down to see his finger bleeding.

With tears brimming in his eyes, Sam whispered, "But I'm your friend." The creature pushed at Sam with his nose. Sam reached his hand out again. Closing his eyes, he began to pet the creature again. This time, the creature licked his hand.

When Sam heard the bag zip, he put his hand back under the blanket and looked up as Trevor turned. Trevor glared at Sam for a minute, and then at the creature who sat next to him. He went upstairs and the wolf lay down next to the cage, waiting. The day dragged for Sam and he was hungry.

It was late in the day when Trevor came back downstairs. "Forget the boy," Trevor said to the wolf. "We need to prepare to leave. It's not safe here for us anymore. Come, we'll take care of this later. "

The creature followed Trevor up the stairs. Sam sat holding his breath listening to the sound of the footsteps overhead. When he heard the door close, he called to Meg.

"Meg," he shouted. "Can you hear me?"

"Yes," she said in a muffled voice. "Did they leave?"

"I think so. What should I do?"

"I remembered something about the ritual. It takes four women. So, if we can just get one person to leave, Trevor can't do anything. So call out to the others and see if anyone is awake."

"I don't think that's going to work. I think…"

"Sam, don't argue with me. Just yell and see if anyone can hear you."

"Okay. Can anyone hear me? Hello. Is anyone awake?" Sam yelled. He heard movement behind one of the doors.

"Hey, lady, can you hear me?" Sam yelled.

"Who's there?" a soft voice asked.

"My name is Sam. Can you open your door? I don't think it's locked."

"Where am I?"

"Don't worry about that right now. Just try and see if you can open the door."

Sam listened to the sound of scraping. He began to feel hopeful as he listened to her feeling around on the walls. She fumbled with the door knob and with a screech the door opened. Sam looked surprised as the lady stumbled blinking at the bright light in the interior room.

"You're the missing boy?" she asked.

"I'm Sam Craig. There's other women down here too."

"Hey, over here," Meg yelled.

"Who's that," the lady asked Sam.

"Her name is Meg. She's a cop," he replied.

"Meg Riley?" she asked surprised.

"Yes," Meg's muffled voice said. "You need to get out and go for help. My door is locked and this man is going to come back to kill us."

The woman walked over to Meg's door and tried the handle. "Meg, it's me, Trudy. I was taken from the station."

"Trudy?" Meg said questioning. "Trudy! Listen, get out of this house. I don't know where we are, but find the nearest house and call Bennett."

"Wait," Sam said, dismissing what Meg was saying. "I know where we are. We are at the end of Dunning Road. The guy who lives here is my neighbor, Trevor Grant. He plans on killing all of us regardless if you are gone or not. I messed up."

Trudy looked at Sam and then back at Meg's door. Sam stood up and let the blanket drop on the floor. "I know I'm only a kid. You probably just want to listen to Meg because she's a grown up. But please, the other two ladies aren't locked in either. Trevor's been giving them drugs. If they can go with you, get them out."

Trudy nodded and walked to the first door. She opened it and saw a woman lying on a dirty mattress. She went and tried to get her to respond. Sam stood watching until she came out alone.

"She's not conscious. I think she needs medical help."

"Then try the other girl. She cries a lot, but I think she's okay."

Trudy went to the next door and opened it. She roused Lauren and helped her to her feet. As they came out of the room, Sam said, "Get out of here quickly. My house is just down the road. It's starting to get dark, so stay out of the woods. The creature may be watching."

"What creature?" Lauren said trembling. Sam looked around and then picked up his blanket.

"He won't hurt you if you're my friends. If you take my blanket, he'll know to let you go."

"Look, Sam," Trudy said. "This isn't a game. You're scaring us."

"I'm serious," Sam said stoically. "He will hurt you unless he knows that I trust you. Take my blanket. He will smell me on it and know that I'm letting you go."

When Trudy hesitated, Sam started crying. "Please, if you don't get out of here, you will be killed. Just take the stupid blanket and get out of here. Now, before he comes back."

Meg had been trying to say something, and finally Trudy heard her, "There is a creature. Listen to Sam. Get out of here."

Trudy took the blanket from Sam's hands and started for the stairs with Lauren leaning on her.

"Hurry," Sam said in exasperation. "It will be for nothing if you get caught." That made the two women move a little faster, but not fast enough for Sam. "Please God. If you are listening. Let them get away. Don't let them die because I told my dad about the creature."

Sam sat down and listened to them walking above him. He heard the door open and close. But he kept praying, even while Meg kept calling out to him.

CHAPTER 47

Reggie was standing in the doorway when the car pulled up. His arms crossed across his large stomach. Jake tensed when he saw the scowl on Reggie's face. Reggie watched as Jake parked the car and got out. Greg glanced at Jake as he opened the door and stepped out. When they reached the door, Reggie didn't move. He looked at both of them and finally spoke.

"I want to see you both in my office." He turned and stormed away. Greg and Jake did as they were told and found themselves standing before Reggie's oversized desk.

Reggie came in with a mug of hot black coffee and sat down in his chair. It groaned under his weight. "Officer Matthew, do you care to explain why I never got a phone call?"

"I tried to tell Peterson that you wanted us to come back or to call, but he wouldn't listen. I told him that you wanted us back at the station. But he insisted on going up the road to talk to the Craig's neighbor about some dog. And then he went to a bunch of other places. I kept telling him we needed to get back."

"Why didn't you call me back and tell me?"

"I think that he's obsessing like Riley, and I didn't want to be a part of that." Reggie looked at Jake. "Is this true, Detective?"

"Not quite. Stanley mentioned that before Sam was missing that first time, he told his father about some weird animal in the woods. Stanley told Sam he would check with this neighbor who claimed it was his dog. But the weird thing was the animal's eyes. Stanley looked it up online and found something that was tied to folklore. So, I thought we'd better check this guy out before we came back here."

"Why before you talked to me?"

"Because of Meg's notes on the creature and Pastor Walt describing the same animal. I just was thinking that if there is a chance that these women and Sam are still alive, I didn't want to waste time."

"But you did waste time, didn't you?"

"I heard a dog growl at the house. So, I wanted to see if anyone in the neighborhood had seen the animal. I just wanted to dig further."

Reggie's chair groaned as he leaned forward. He looked back at Jake. "I know that I asked you to come back and help. But you are here under my authority. I have some information that was crucial to this case and you're off on some side trip."

"I understand. I was just thinking it was getting late. If this guy is going to make a move, it will be at night."

"Maybe we should investigate this guy, not antagonize him," Greg said in a huff.

"Matthews, why don't you see if Marty is back yet. I want to talk to Jake alone for a minute." Greg left and closed the door behind him.

"Reggie, I went up to that house to see if there was probable cause to see if Judge Murphy would give us a search warrant."

"But you didn't get anything. Did you?" Reggie asked.

"No," Jake said gloomily. "I hate the thought of another night with these people missing."

"And that's why you shouldn't have wasted your time. Did you ever check on that Shamus O'Leary that was in Riley's file?"

"As soon I got back yesterday. There was nothing in the system for him. She checked too and found nothing."

"I went and talked to Mo Reynolds. O'Leary is the one that rented the old Hanson place."

"But that's where Trevor is living. Then who is Trevor?"

"Claims to be O'Leary's nephew."

"But I didn't see any O'Leary. Where is he now?"

"He took a flight out of Albany for Dublin last week. I called the authorities in Dublin and had a very interesting phone call that puts new light on this case. O'Leary was turned over to the authorities as he stepped off the plane. Seems he wanted to make amends with the family because he is elderly now. But the daughter was aware that some 30 years ago, her father had abducted a boy. They had tried to have him arrested back then, but he fled the country."

"Thirty years ago? Certainly the statute of limitations is up on that case?" Jake said.

"Probably. But he is also wanted in connection with some crimes in London."

"London?"

"You must have read about them yesterday. They are the same ones in Riley's file. The same ones that have the matching hairs to our cases."

"Meg was on the right track."

"Oh, it gets better. The name of the boy he abducted is Trevor."

Jake felt like the wind was knocked out of him. "You mean, Trevor is the child that was abducted?"

"And if he is, his mother is still living. She's never stopped looking for him. O'Leary's health is failing. He wanted to see his great grandchild before he died. So, they made a deal. He told them everything about the abduction in exchange for seeing the family."

"We better get back over…," Jake interrupted.

"Jake, we are going to do this by the book. I'm waiting for the search warrant now that we have probable cause."

Jake sank down into a chair. "So, did O'Leary…"

"Nope," Reggie said shaking his head. "Only about a 30 year old kidnapping that he can't be tried for. We need to see if we can come up with enough evidence to pin him as an accomplice in our kidnappings."

"An accomplice? If Trevor was that little boy, he can't be responsible for all this…can he?"

"He has to be in his forties by now. But it's not up to us to judge his mental capacity. It's up to us to arrest the person or persons responsible for all that has happened here in Granelle. Have you decided if you're going to stay on the force when this is all over?"

Jake looked surprised at the change in subject and then shook his head, "I'm going back to the church. I want to serve the Lord and I feel I can do that better from behind a pulpit."

"Okay," Reggie said sitting back in his chair. "Then I can tell you something, but it's just between us. Got it?"

"Sure," Jake said with a shrug.

"I was wrong about Riley. I'm only admitting that I made a mistake to you because I won't be your boss when this is all over."

"Reggie, you don't need to do this," Jake started.

"Yeah, I do. When she started talking about folklore and werewolves, it reminded me of when you got religious. I didn't want her to go in that direction. Instead of looking at what she was trying to show me objectively, I got hot and told her off. I was wrong. There is some Irish folklore about a creature that lived forever and their keepers. O'Leary believes that he was a keeper and turned those powers over to Trevor. Can't prove it yet, but it's all connected, even to Angelos."

"So, what happens to Angelos now?"

"Let's take this one case at a time. My theory is that they were trying to get another boy. Sam."

There was a knock on the door. Greg walked in with a paper in his hand. "We got the search warrant."

"By the book, Jake," Reggie got up and took the warrant from Greg.

CHAPTER 48

Trudy and Lauren clung to each other as they walked down the side of the road in the growing darkness with Sam's blanket draped over Lauren's shoulders. Trudy walked next to the woods and felt something shadowing them. She turned a few times, but couldn't see anything in the dark woods. In the isolation of the long stretch of woods between the houses, every noise seemed menacing. Trudy knew that somewhere out there was their abductor.

As they turned a corner, the glow from a house could be seen in the distance. Lauren seemed buoyed by the light and began to pick up her pace. But so did the rushing noise next to Trudy.

"Slow down," Trudy whispered. "We want to make it there."

Lauren slowed a bit. Trudy glanced beside her and saw two glowing eyes staring back. She gasped.

"What is it?" Lauren said in a frightened voice.

Trudy tried to swallow, but her throat was dry. Lauren looked into the woods and saw nothing. Trudy stopped walking and stared at the dark spot in the woods. Lauren pulled at her. "Come on," she said. "We're almost there."

Trudy started walking again and saw the shadow move with them. Lauren, feeling Trudy's unease, began to cry.

"Shhh," Trudy said. "It's alright. We're friends of Sam's…right?"

"What?" Lauren said through her tears.

"Nothing. Just keep going," Trudy said. They stumbled closer to the light down the road. Lauren's sobs subsided to heavy breathing. As they neared the Craig's property, a sharp whistle filled the night. Trudy glanced to her right and saw the eyes looking right at her. Lauren saw them, too. As she drew a deep breath to scream, Trudy clamped her hand over Lauren's mouth.

"Don't scream. He will find us," she whispered. She dragged Lauren toward the detached garage, praying that it was unlocked. The dark shadow kept pace. Lauren struggled to pull away from Trudy.

"Don't be a fool. You'll get us killed. I'm a cop, remember," Trudy whispered harshly, practically shaking Lauren. "If you understand me, nod."

When Lauren nodded, Trudy let her go and reached out for the door. The dark shadow growled. Much to Trudy's relief, Lauren passed out. Trudy pulled opened the side door of the garage and dragged Lauren inside with her. The sharp whistle pierced the air again. As she pulled the door closed and locked it, Trudy looked out the window in the door and watched as the dark shadow ran away into the woods.

"Thanks, Sam," she whispered. "I think you just saved our lives."

CHAPTER 49

Jake drove with the siren on as he sped back toward Dunning Road. He prayed that they weren't too late, while praying for safety. He didn't know that at Granelle Gospel, a prayer vigil had been ongoing for the missing women and Sam, with special prayers going up for the pastor, who was on loan to the police department.

Reggie told Greg about O'Leary as Jake drove the familiar route toward the Craig's. He silenced the siren as he approached Dunning Road so they wouldn't warn Trevor. They drove down the dark desolate road in silence. The house was dark when they got there. Greg pulled a flashlight out of the glove box. Jake and Greg walked up to the front door, and Jake knocked. Reggie skirted around the side of the house toward the shed.

"Trevor Grant. This is the Granelle Police Department. We have a warrant to search the premises," Jake called out. Jake waited for a moment. No one answered. The house was dark. Jake knocked again as he gestured to Greg to stand to the side. Jake waited a few moments and then turned the door handle. He was surprised to find it was unlocked. Jake pulled his gun out and pushed the door open with it.

"Trevor Grant, this is the Granelle Police Department. We have a warrant to search the premises," Jake called out inside the house. There was no response. Jake cautiously entered the house and heard noise from the back of the house. Figuring it was Reggie, he moved forward into the living room. He saw the empty dusty room and knew that Trevor hadn't lived in this part of the house. Jake walked down the narrow hall next to the staircase toward the back of the house. There was a door in the hallway and Jake paused next to it listening. Jake motioned for Greg to check the upstairs rooms.

Jake slowly opened the door and a dim light spilled onto the stairs. The stairs were boxed in on both sides with concrete blocks. Jake had no cover at the bottom of the stairs. He called out a warning again and slowly walked down the stairs. He gripped his gun tight with his finger on the trigger. He got to the bottom of the stairs and there was a small room that was empty. Jake looked to his right and saw another hallway leading to another room.

"Trevor Grant, this is your last warning. Come out," Jake called out.

"Hey, we're down here," a voice called out.

"Are you alone?" Jake asked cautiously walking down the narrow hallway. Every muscle was tense and Jake was suddenly nervous. It had been a lot of years since he was in this position, and he was unsure of himself.

"It's just the three of us," the voice called out desperately. "Hurry, before he comes back."

Jake looked around the corner into the room. He saw Meg and Sam locked in a cage. Meg looked like she was sleeping.

"Pastor Jake?" Sam asked. "Is that really you?"

"Yes, Sam it's really me. Where's Trevor?"

"He went out a little while ago. He was mad because two of the women got away. He sent the creature out to find them."

"Is anyone else here but you and Det. Riley?"

"There is still someone in one of the rooms."

Jake quickly looked in each room and found Martha Rowley on a dirty mattress. He checked her vitals and found her alive.

"Sam…" Jake started. A large crash from upstairs startled them both. He put his finger to his mouth to warned Sam to be quiet. Sam nodded and sat down on the floor. He wrapped a dirty blanket around his shoulders. Jake leaned up against the wall near the hallway. He glanced down the hall and saw nothing. He could hear noises from overhead.

"Be careful," Sam whispered. "He can be mean."

Jake nodded and gestured for Sam to be quiet. Jake began to quietly walk back down the hall toward the little room. As he got to the stairs to look up, his weapon was knocked from his hand. He went to react, but saw a large wolf on the stairs. The fur on its back was standing up and it started to growl at Jake. Jake stood still as Trevor leaned down and picked up the gun.

"Well, we meet again," Trevor said as he motioned with the gun for Jake to go back down the hall. Jake walked backwards afraid to take his eyes off the wolf. He backed up to the cage. As Jake bumped the cage, Meg roused and began to sit up. Trevor smiled as the wolf walked up and sniffed Jake.

"That's right," Trevor said setting the gun down on a workbench. "He is next. But I want to have a little fun first."

The wolf walked around the cage to where Sam was and laid down. Meg tried to reach out and pull Sam toward her, but he reached out a hand to the wolf. She watched horrified as the wolf licked Sam's hand before he pulled it back in the cage.

"It's not too late for you, Trevor," Jake started.

"Not too late," Trevor mimicked and then laughed. "It's too late for you. Should have stayed at the church. You were safer there."

"We know about O'Leary. This isn't all your fault."

"What do you think you know about my uncle?" Trevor said as he turned his back to Jake. Jake took a step and the wolf growled.

"Be careful," Sam whispered.

"Yes, listen to the boy," Trevor said looking at Sam. "Such a disappointment he has been so far. But he is right. You definitely aren't my friend and he will kill you at my command."

"Okay," Jake said stepping back toward the cage. "But we know that O'Leary isn't your uncle."

"Oh and how do you know that?" Trevor asked turning around to face Jake. He crossed his arms defiantly.

"Well, since when is Trevor Grant an Irish name?"

"My mother was Irish and my father French. Besides, wasting time won't matter. Everything went wrong. Now, I'm going to have to kill you all."

"O'Leary talked to the police in Ireland. We know that he abducted you as a child. You aren't related to him at all."

"You're a liar," Trevor yelled. "He is my uncle. My parents didn't want me so I lived with him."

"No," Jake said in a gentle voice. "He told the police the truth in exchange for seeing his daughter. She turned him into the police. You've been missing since you were a boy."

Trevor went up to Jake and slammed him into the cage. "Shut up!" he yelled. "You don't know anything. You're just a stupid failure as a cop. You put Doug in jail for doing nothing. You're a failure!"

Jake put his hands up to defend himself, but saw the wolf jump to its feet. Jake saw Sam reach out his hand and stop it. "Listen, Trevor, your parents searched for years for you. Your mother is still alive in France. She never stopped hoping you would come home."

Trevor was shaking in anger. "No, the only family I have is Shamus. We've been with the creatures all these years. It is our destiny to care for them and help them survive. We have a special gift from them to live forever. I have that gift because I'm Shamus's son. Just like Sam was to be my son." Trevor turned his wrath on Sam. "But you are a disappointment. You told them about me. Now look what you have done!"

Trevor walked back to the bench and picked up Jake's gun. He waved it at Jake and then at Meg. "Yes, I'll start with you. Because I know the cop still loves you," he said pointing the gun at Meg. He looked over at Jake. "Haven't you figured it out yet?"

Jake nodded. "You chose Meg because she was my ex-partner and Trudy because she works for the force."

"See, still stupid aren't you. How did you become a detective? Everyone is tied to you. Every person I chose. From your ex-*girlfriend* to this kid."

"No," Jake said slowly. "Not everyone is connected to me. How is Lauren Stewart or Martha Rowley connected?"

He waved the gun and laughed again. "Stupid man. Martha Rowley is a member of your church. Lauren Stewart is Jessie Buchanan's niece."

"Martha Rowley isn't a member and how do you know that Lauren is Jessie's niece?"

"They are on your church rolls! This is getting us nowhere. It's time to just end this before someone comes looking for you." Trevor reached up for a key to open the cage. Jake looked at Sam who nodded and he rushed up and grabbed Trevor. The wolf growled but didn't move. The two men wrestled with the gun and it fell on the floor spinning out of reach. Trevor grabbed a wrench off the workbench and hit Jake with it making him fall on the floor.

"Kill him," Trevor yelled at the wolf. The wolf ran around the cage toward Jake.

"No," Sam yelled. The wolf stopped and looked at Sam and then back over to Trevor.

"Kill him," Trevor said.

"And I say no. I'm the keeper now. Did you forget?" The boy lifts his hand and showed the fresh wound on his finger.

Trevor laughed. "That means nothing. Shamus still had power over the beasts. I have been the keeper for a long time. I control the beast. I'll kill all of you. I'll find another boy."

"Shamus didn't have the power of the beast," Jake said. "This power doesn't exist. It's just a myth." The wolf began to growl.

"That's not true," Trevor, said a little unsure.

"Kill him," Sam said in quiet voice, pointing at Trevor. The wolf turned away from Jake and slothfully walked toward Trevor.

"No," Trevor yelled. "Kill the preacher. I'm the keeper. I've protected you…." The wolf jumped at Trevor knocking him to the ground. Trevor kept yelling while the wolf attacked him. Meg pulled Sam to her, shielding his eyes from the grisly scene. Jake went for his gun. The wolf turned and growled, looking at Jake.

Sam pulled away from Meg. "No," he yelled. "He is not prey. Leave him to me." The wolf hesitated. "I said…LEAVE."

The wolf ran out of the room. Jake picked up his gun and went to go after the animal. "No," Sam said. "He won't hurt you. Not as long as you're my friend."

"What do you mean, Sam?" Meg asked.

"Nothing," Sam said shaking his head. "Nothing. It was something Trevor said to me a long time ago. I just want to go home." He put his hand on Meg's shoulder. "Can you take me home to my dad now?"

Meg hesitated looking in Sam's eye. Finally she nodded. "Sure. Jake…" She turned to see Jake leaning over Trevor.

"Is he…?" Meg asked.

"No, he's still alive, but hurt. Let me get help. I'll have to go upstairs. But I'm not leaving you two down here with him."

"The key is on the top shelf," Sam said pointing to the shelf above the work bench.

Jake unlocked the door to the cage and Sam threw his arms around him. "I knew you would come. I prayed and God finally answered one of my prayers."

Jake patted Sam's back and looked at Meg questioning. She shrugged and walked over to Jake, too. Jake reached out and pulled her into his hug with Sam. For a few moments, they just stood together.

"Come on. I don't trust that wolf, and Trevor may come around. I need to find Reggie and Greg and see if they are okay." Jake led them out of the room. Meg faltered and Jake picked her up and carried her upstairs.

CHAPTER 50

After getting Meg and Sam upstairs, Jake found Reggie locked in the shed and broke the lock to get him out. Reggie radioed for an ambulance and then searched for Greg. He found him barely conscious from a head wound and handcuffed in an upstairs bedroom. Jake went back to the basement to check on Trevor. He hadn't moved, but the wounds on his shoulder were bleeding badly. He applied pressure to the wounds and waited for help to come. A few minutes later, Jake heard sirens and the slamming of doors. He heard muffled voices upstairs and waited for someone to come.

Jake heard someone on the stairs, "Peterson, you down there?"

"Just keep coming, Reggie," Jake replied.

Reggie had to stoop as he came through the small doorway. "This the guy?" he asked.

"Yes, this is Trevor Grant. And in that small room over there is Martha Rowley," Jake said as he pointed to the opened door. Reggie went in and checked on her.

"She looks about like Kathy Stanwick did when we found her," Reggie said. He yelled upstairs for help.

"You're going to need a few ambulances. I think Meg and Sam are going to need to be checked out, too."

"Don't worry about that. I've got it covered. What about you?"

"Me?" Jake asked surprised. "I'm fine."

"Okay, get handcuffs on him," Reggie said gesturing at Trevor. Jake started to say something. But Reggie silenced him. "We don't want to take any chances. This guy may have an insanity defense, but he's still calculating and cunning."

Jake nodded and cuffed Trevor's hands in front. Reggie stood there watching as Jake applied pressure to the wounds again.

"So, what now, Jake?"

"I'm going back to the church."

"No hesitation? No second thoughts?"

"I thought I missed police work. But I think it was just this case. There were so many loose ends from my last case. Plus he hurt people that I care about. I just wanted to help anyway I could."

"I've asked you this before. You don't think God can use you as a cop?"

"I'm sure He can. But in spite of all the really hard work of being a minister, I love helping the people. I just need Pastor Walt to show me how to make it all work."

Reggie nodded as two EMT's came into the small room. Jake stepped back and watched for a moment before going back upstairs. Lights from the ambulances and police cruisers lit up the room with flashing lights. Meg was lying on a stretcher and being wheeled out onto the porch and she motioned to Jake. He came over and knelt next to the stretcher.

"I thought when I saw you come in with your gun that you were back…" she stopped as her voice broke. Jake reached out and she pushed his arm away. "Don't…"

"Meg…"

"Just let me finish. I thought you were back. That you came back for me. But I know that you came back for Sam."

"It wasn't just about Sam. It was you…and Trudy. She was kidnapped because of me."

Meg nodded. "It's over, that's all that matters."

"You were right, you know. All the cases are connected and O'Leary and Grant were responsible."

"Thanks. I needed to hear that. Hopefully, Bennett agrees," she said closing her eyes with a slight smile. Jake nodded to the EMT's who took the stretcher down the steps to the waiting ambulance.

Sam sat on the couch being checked over and looked up at Jake. He went over and smiled down at him. "How are you?"

"I'm okay, Pastor Jake. I keep telling them that. I just want to go home to my Dad."

"Okay, I'll take you." Jake put his hand out and Sam slipped his small one into his. Jake led him out to one of the police cars and put him in. He gestured to Reggie who was talking to Matthews and Reggie nodded.

"All set?" Jake said and Sam just nodded. He looked tired and still a bit scared. It was a quick trip down the road to his house.

Jake drove the car up in front of the Craig's house. "Well, bud, you're home. Should we see where your Dad is?"

Sam hesitated, "Pastor Jake? Are you going to be a cop now?"

"No," Jake replied. "I'll be back at church. I've got a lot of work to catch up on."

"Do you think God minded that you went back to being a cop for a little bit?"

"I think God was fine with it. It had to be, I found you. Come on, let's see your father. He's been really worried about you."

"Okay," Sam said opening the door. As Jake got out, Stanley was coming out the door with a surprised look.

"Sam?" Stanley said hesitantly. "Is it really you?

Sam ran and hugged his father and both were in tears. Jake waited to give them a few minutes, then he walked over to talk to Stanley. Jake watched as Sam clung to his father.

"Where did you find him?" Stanley asked.

"He was being held by Trevor Grant in his basement along with two of the missing women."

"Trevor...our neighbor. But why?"

"Dad," Sam's voice was muffled against his father. "I told the other two ladies to come here. Didn't they make it?"

"Here?" Stanley looked at Jake. "I didn't see anyone."

Jake knelt down in front of Sam. "Was it Trudy and Lauren?"

Sam looked at Jake and nodded. "Maybe they're in the garage..."

Jake looked up at the detached garage and took off running. Once there he looked into the dark windows. Then he called out, "Trudy, its Jake can you hear me?" He went to the side door and twisted the handle. Stanley came up beside him and pulled keys out of his pocket. He pulled opened the door and turned on a light. Huddled together against the back wall, Trudy and Lauren held each other under Sam's dirty blanket.

Lauren started crying as Jake ran over to the women. Pulling them to their feet, Jake and Stanley led them to the house. A few minutes later, Reggie was talking to Trudy as EMT's loaded Lauren into the ambulance.

Jake stood looking at the woods. He knew somewhere out there, the wolf was hiding. But Sam was safe and would be leaving in the morning for

Poughkeepsie. He was sure Stanley wouldn't let Sam out of his sight for a long time. Jake got into the car and drove down the quiet wooded street, and he realized just how isolated this road had been.

After a quiet drive, he pulled up in front of a familiar house. He looked across the street at the cross that lit up the side of the church. Pastor Walt opened the front door of the parsonage and waited for Jake.

"Pastor Walt, it's over. We found the women and Sam is home safe with Stanley," Jake said as he walked up the lawn to the door.

"We've been praying continually and I see that those prayers have been answered."

"Keep on praying. The women have been through quite an ordeal. We found two of them locked in a basement with Sam over on Dunning Road. The other two had managed to get away and were hiding in the Craig's garage. Now, they are all at the hospital getting checked over."

Jake looked up surprised to see Millie standing right behind Pastor Walt. "Come on in. I'm sure you haven't had a good meal in you in days."

Walt chuckled. "Just like Millie. Always needs to take care of people. You can't say no. We'll be right in, dear." Millie nodded and went back inside to get food ready for Jake. "So, did you find the animal?"

"Yes, but it got away. I went for my gun, but Sam called me off and it ran away."

"What kind of animal was it?"

"It was like a big wolf, but not really. It was strange."

"What about the man?"

"The animal attacked him. But he's still alive. I imagine he will be going to jail. I feel bad though. We had just found out that this guy had been abducted as a child and raised by a man who lived with these animals. Apparently, he was trying to do the same with Sam."

"At least Sam is safe now."

"And we don't have to worry about the animal getting to him. Stanley is leaving in the morning to join his daughter in Poughkeepsie."

"Good. Now what about you? You ready to come back?"

"Absolutely. But I have one more thing I need to do first. I need to talk to the DA about getting Angelos released to a hospital to help him deal with his mental issues. I'm going to go down and see him too. Let him know I'm sorry for my part in the whole thing."

Millie called from inside. Walt chuckled, "Come on. Before she comes looking for us. She still thinks I should be in bed."

The wolf sat in the woods watching the two men as the door closed behind them. As the porch light went off, the wolf turned and headed back into the woods.

* * *

It was spring in the Adirondack Mountains. Just inside the wood line, a female wolf protectively drew her two young pups near her. The male who had lured her away from her pack stood with his back to them smelling the air. As soon as the pups were weaned he began to drive the small family south. She trembled as he turned and looked at her. The male pup trotted away from her protection and sat down next to its father. The wolf looked down at the pup and then sniffed the air again. The female knew that they would be moving again soon.

The further south they went, the more people were around and that scared the female more. She lived in constant fear. She didn't know what the strange grey path was, nor did she know what the cars were that were filled with the smells of humans. It seemed strange to her that the male stayed close to the path and even looked at the big green signs on the side from time to time. The male began to move and the female sighed as she rose to follow. She glanced at the green sign and didn't know that it read Poughkeepsie 30 miles.